We Get Our Living
Like Milk from the Land

Edited
Lee Maracle
Jeannette C. Armstrong
Delphine Derickson
Greg Young-Ing

Researched and Compiled by
The Okanagan Rights Committee
and
The Okanagan Indian Education Resource Society

Canadian Cataloguing in Publication Data
Main entry under title: We get our living like milk from the land

ISBN 0-919441-36-X
1. Okanagan Indians—History. 2. Indians of North America—British Columbia-History I. Armstrong, Jeannette C. II. Okanagan Rights Committee. III. Okanagan Indian Education Resource Society.
E99.035W4 1993   971.1'004979   C94-910063-3

The Publisher wishes to acknowledge the support of Canada Council and Cultural Services Branch of the Province of British Columbia in the publication of this book.

This book is not intended for use in legal purposes and is not authorized as legal or binding in any exception whatsoever. Although extreme care has been taken to ensure that all information in this book is accurate, the author nor the publisher can be held legally responsible for any errors that may appear.

Editors: Lee Maracle, Jeannette C. Armstrong, Delphine Derickson, Greg Young-Ing

Cover Art: Casey Dennis

Book Design/Typesetting: Troy D. Hunter

Photo's: Archives, British Columbia and Canada, Phillip Collection, Armstrong Collection

Printed and bound in Canada.

TABLE OF CONTENTS

PREFACE

The Okanagan Tribal Council made a commitment to establish a democratic process which would facilitate the resolution of the outstanding "Land Question Issue." Consequently, in 1988, the Okanagan Tribal Council initiated a process which would result in the production of an historical booklet which would outline, the pre-contact history, the history of colonization and contemporary history.

The purpose of the booklet was to provide an historically factual basis for all the grassroots members of the Okanagan Nation. In this regard the Okanagan Tribal Council agreed to organize and conduct a series of workshops to discuss:

1. The history of the Okanagan Nation in terms of where we come from

2. The history of the Okanagan Nation in terms of what happened to us

3. The present day history of the Okanagan Nation in terms of where we go from here.

Members of the Okanagan Nation recognized the need for the active involvement of all the Okanagan people in setting the future direction of the Nation.

Therefore, it is with great pride that we acknowledge our collective achievement in completing the initial phase of our stated consultation process. We would like to take this opportunity to commend the efforts of the many committed and dedicated individuals who have successfully overcome many difficulties in order that the Okanagan people may begin the process of telling their story.

JOAN C. PHILLIP
Executive Director
Okanagan Tribal Council

OKANAGAN ELDERS STATEMENTS

I am encouraged that this book has been completed. It is to be for education and historical information purposes. The book is not to be used for negotiations on Okanagan Land Claims. We wish it to be a tool to help protect our land and our rights.

LOUISE GABRIEL
Spokesperson and President of Okanagan Elders Council
November 1993

This is the Creator's Land. It is our lifeblood. We are here to defend the land. Our situation is now risky. Everyone needs to know what the history really is. I am encouraged when my people defend the land. We have a right to be Okanagan. The Creator gave us that right. We have looked after that right by looking after the land. We cannot stop. Be brave because the future needs us to be.
(translated from Okanagan)

TOMMY GREGOIRE
Spokesperson of Confederated Okanagan Shuswap Traditional Alliance
October 1993

ORIGINAL PEOPLE

The original people of the Okanagan are known as the syilx speaking people. They have been here since the beginning of people on this land.

The original people of the Okanagan were wished here by k̓ʷləncútən, the Creator of oneself, Creator and arranger of the world.

The syilx people know history, passed on from one person to another, from generation to generation, as a record called cəpcaptík̓ʷł. It is a history of the meaning of being syilx, rather than a history of dates. The **meanings** in the cəpcaptík̓ʷł are formed through story. They are the truths and knowledge of the natural laws made active through story.

In the cəpcaptík̓ʷł we are told that k̓ʷləncútən, created and sent sənk̓ĺip, Coyote, to help change things so that our people might survive on the earth. Coyote's travels across the land are a record of the natural laws our people learned in order to survive.

Learning and teaching the natural laws on the land is necessary for humans to live and to continue on. Humans don't have instinct to know how to live in nature's laws. They were given memory instead. Understanding the living land and teaching how to be part of that is the only way we, the syilx, have survived.

High Mountain Cloud, Head of the Lake Band, Vernon, B.C.

Provincial Archives Photo.

st̓əlsqílxʷ was the beginning of people on this land.   st̓əlsqílxʷ slowly changed to become the sqilxʷ, the original people of this land. They became changed through learning to live on the land. The cəpcaptíkʷɬ tell of four stages of learning that they went through. All our laws come from these four stages of learning.

The first law is to understand and to live in balance with the natural world. This first law has been put into the meanings in the cəpcaptíkʷɬ.

The other laws are for people to get along with each other in a healthy way and for passing on ways which are respectful to all creation. We govern ourselves by these laws. These are the four stages.

1) st̓əlsqílxʷ (torn from the earth sqilxʷ) life form of first people without natural instincts to survive

2) xatma?sqílxʷ (in front of us sqilxʷ) first thinking people who learned the natural law to survive

3) sqilxʷ (dreaming ones, bound together, of the land) original people who learned to live together on the land in peace

4) ?awtma?sqílxʷ (to struggle and/or come after sqilxʷ) today's sqilxʷ after the arrival of newcomers

(note. these interpretations are based on root words meanings in the syllables of each word)

The language which arose from our learning about the land is called the syilx language. All who speak it are called the syilx because the language carries the teachings of a very old civilization with thousands of years of knowledge of healthy living on this land. The laws are always taught by telling the stories to each child and to any adults who need reminding.

The land forms in the stories are teachings and are reminders to each generation, that the land is at the centre of how we are to behave. The destruction of the story land marks and natural land forms are like tearing pages out of a history book to the syilx. Without land knowledge we are endangered as a life form on that land and we in turn endanger other life forms there.

The syilx speaking people's lands lie on both sides of the Okanagan River, east to the Selkirk range, west to the Cascades summit, south into Washington bounded by the Columbia River and Lake Chelan and north up to Salmon River.

The syilx Territory had eight organized districts. All speak syilx and have the same customs and stories. They are one Nation and are now commonly called the Okanagan.

These are:
Southern Okanagan or sənq'aʔitkʷ
Northern Okanagan or suknaqínx
San Poil or sənpʕʷílx
Colville/ Kettle or sənx̌ʷyaʔɬpítkʷ
Arrow Lakes or sʔaltʼíkʷət
Slocan or sənʕíckstx
Similkameen/Methow or sməlqmíx

4

ORIGINAL OKANAGAN TERRITORY

(Approximate Boundary)

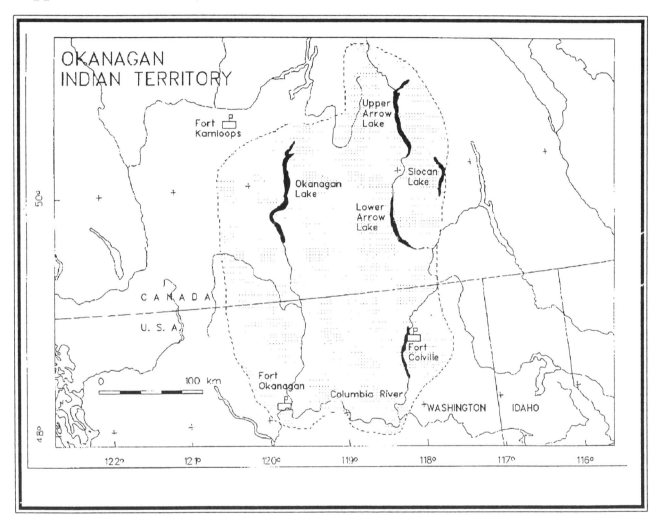

The Northern Okanagan, suknaqínx, occupy the lands in the Okanagan Valley north of Oroville and include the Douglas Lake area. The sənx̌ʷyaʔɬpítkʷ, Kettle, occupy the Kettle Valley to the Great Kettle Falls. The sʔaltʼíkʷət, Arrow Lakes, occupy the Arrow Lakes down to Kettle Falls. The sənʕíckstx, Slocan, occupy the Slocan down to Chewelah. The sməlqmíx occupy the Similkameen Valley from Princeton to the south bordered by the Methow. The San Poil, sənpʕʷílx, occupying the San Poil River to where it meets with the Columbia river. The Southern Okanagan, sənq'aʔitkʷ, occupy the lands surrounding the Okanagan River to where it meets with the Columbia.

The suknaqínx, the sənʕickstx, the sʔalt̓ik̓ʷət, and part of the sənx̌ʷyaʔɬpítkʷ and sməlqmíx are traditional districts which are now part of the territory north of the Canada/USA boundary.

Before European invasion, the syilx moved freely between the south, north, west, and eastern parts of their territory. The syilx people had a very well organized system. They were organized by how the land was used for survival in the syilx

MAP SHOWING NORTHERN DISTRICTS IN CANADA

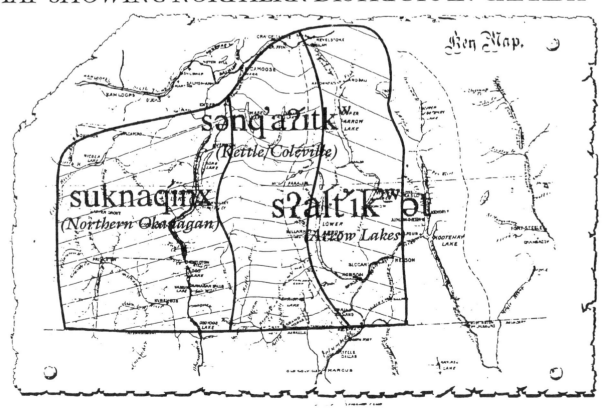

6

cultural traditions. The land was used for hunting, fishing, root digging and berry picking. The traditional food gathering areas were shared by all the syilx. Some territories were also shared with other friendly tribes.

The syilx organized themselves in order to protect and practice our rights. The **right** to live and survive as a syilx is where all our rights come from. Living our rights brought us to this time in our history.

Freedom within our territory is a right coming out of having looked after the land for thousands of years without destroying it. The syilx preserved the land in its natural healthy state for each generation through knowledge and the practise of natural law. Because of that we are still here. We have the right to live on the bounty which our ancestors passed down to us as pure as when the Creator gave it. It is the same as inheriting a house or money which your parents worked and saved for. No guns, nor foreign laws on paper of other people, who destroyed their own land, can change that truth.

All of syilx territory is marked with our signs. The land is understood in how to survive on it. Our people, all carry the right to be syilx because of that. Their right is a responsibility to the **future**.

The way the people together carry out their rights, as governing groups, are what the nation, district and village chieftainships were organized for.

It is each person's right to live in any community on the territory as long as the customs and laws are followed by the individual. If a person or family did not follow the laws of a community, they still had the right to live alone on the land and survive.

The right of being a **syilx is a responsibility,** first to know and follow the natural laws to make sure of healthy generations to come, and second to follow the laws of a community for the same reason.

The syilx people had good governance through the chieftainship system. The chief represented the will of the people in carrying out the rights of being syilx.

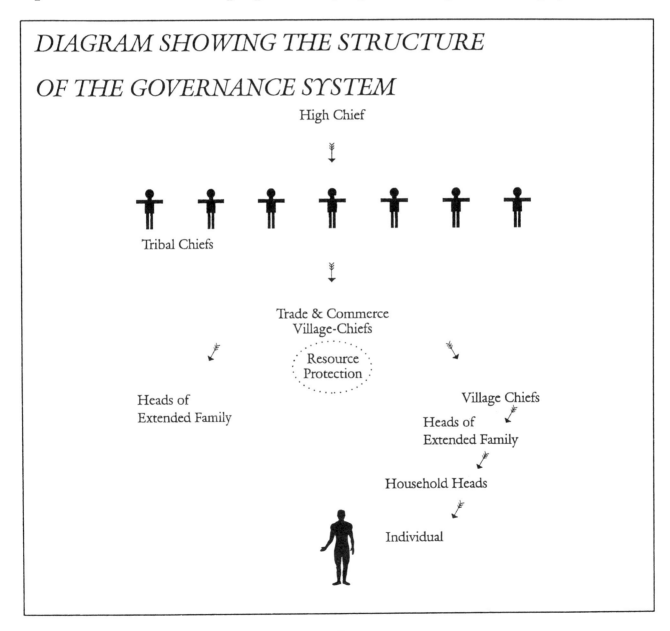

DIAGRAM SHOWING THE STRUCTURE OF THE GOVERNANCE SYSTEM

High Chief

Tribal Chiefs

Trade & Commerce
Village-Chiefs

Resource
Protection

Heads of
Extended Family

Village Chiefs

Heads of
Extended Family

Household Heads

Individual

The chief represented the guarantee that the syilx will continue on. The Chief represented good decisions of the people while protecting the land and the natural laws. It is a responsibility to balance human needs with the natural laws.

The **Protection** of the land and natural resources means the protection of the **coming generations. This** is always the main responsibility of chieftainship in representing the will of the people. The chief is fully responsible to represent the **rights of future** generations and their health, not just **the rights of each person** living in the village.

The chief is the centre of people's strength and was always in emotional, physical, spiritual and mental balance. Most important of all, the chief was a good role model for the youth and all the people.

The syilx people had one High Chief who lived in the Northern Okanagan district at Nkmepelks and who travelled to visit each district. Each district had a head tribal chief and chiefs for each village. All districts cooperated with each other and shared hunting, fishing and food gathering territory, they also inter-married.

A high chief represented the laws of the whole syilx at the nation level to protect the rights of the syilx. The high chief chose and gave his title to one that he trained before his death. The high chief family decided among themselves who could continue the responsibility of carrying the right of all the syilx forward. They are responsible for protecting the land, the people, the language and the syilx ways.

The high chiefs, p'əlk'múla?xʷ, meaning Earth Turning, and later Nkwala and then Chilheetza were called "silwa lh yilmixwem." They were overseers of our right as the syilx. They had the responsibility of territorial protection, inter-nation trading and upheld co-operation with other Nations.

Large districts had a tribal chief. Some large districts had two tribal chiefs. Usually there was the main tribal chief to keep peace between villages and another called a warchief. The warchief was one who watched for enemies from outside their territory. His role was to protect the syilx people.

Tribal chiefs like Whawheylxw, Little Red Fox, of the Arrow Lakes/Slocan oversaw decisions for food allocation for trading with neighbouring friendly tribes, like the Kalispel and the Spokanes. He closely regulated the movement of his villages through the lakes territory because of the constant threat of unfriendly tribes from the east.

Chief John Chilheetza,
Douglas Lake, BC.

Photo courtesy of
National Museums of Canada.

Another example is the high salmon chief at Kettle Falls. Knkannaxwa (died 1896) was a tribal chief who had the say over how many salmon were to be caught at the falls fishery by all the tribes of the syilx. This was done in order that there would always be salmon for all the syilx people.

A village chief represented village concerns at the extended family level to make sure the laws of the village were peacefully kept. Village chiefs were selected from the (katlh) hereditary family of chiefs. The village chief trained several good-minded sons, nephews, grandsons, or even sons-in-law. One of them gradually took over duties while the old chief was still alive. This one would usually become the next chief.

Village chiefs, called yilmixwem had the say about resources on the land in their village areas. For example, in the Ashnola area (near Keremeos B.C.) the village chiefs had the say in the hunting of the big horn sheep, the taking of eagle feathers and the gathering and trading of tulmin (Indian paint) because these things were located in that village's area. It was a responsibility to care for and regulate the use of those things so they would not be over used.

After the death of a village chief, family head elders gathered to confirm the choice. The will of the people is the strength of the Chief. The survival of the people even into the future and the protection of all the life on the land is the only reason for a chief in the community. All other things are everyone's responsibility.

The sənq'aʔitkʷ, Southern Okanagan, practised a good custom in which a village had two or three chiefs at one time, each with equal authority. They took turns in the duty of village chief.

There were women chieftainesses in some of the sənqʼaʔitkʷ Southern Okanagan villages. They were called Skumalt, women of great authority. They were appointed formally at a village meeting just as a chief is. They were always related to the chief, and at death, the office passed to another female relative. As an example in a village near Omak, the chief served as the group manager while the Skumalt was the adviser in cases of serious crimes or emergencies.

In the villages the heads of extended family clans were called xatus meaning "head of". They could be either male or female. Xatus took care of keeping good relations between their family members and other family clans. An example is if a family member did wrong to a person from another family and the household head could not straighten it out, then it went to all the family heads. In a dispute, the responsibility moved upward to the village chief until it was cleared up.

Josephine or Chief Water,
from Douglas Lake, BC.

Photo courtesy National Museums of Canada.

The eldest of each household, called "tlax tla kap" whether female or male, were responsible for the good conduct of individual family members in the day to day work of the households.

Serious older males or females became suxencwiltm, the ones who discipline. They were law keepers who took on a role to keep discipline and peace in the village. They were usually called on to give "reminder" talks at funerals and to talk to young married people who were having problems. Some of the males were later called watchmen and were given duties by the Catholic priests similar to policemen. Later they became advisors to the chief and were called "sux kwina mam" and were called councillors.

Individual members were responsible to the household heads. Each person was free to work at whatever they chose. The responsibility of the individual to the whole village is central to the rights of the individual. Individual rights were very carefully respected as long as they in turn respected the rights of others.

The syilx had a very organized life style. Each member had a responsibility and a part in the way the whole Nation lived in health. They had a good system of day-to-day care of people in the community. Such customs were the same throughout the syilx territory.

Babies up to age three always accompanied the mothers of one family. They worked together and helped each other to feed and care for them. There was never a need for babysitters and leaving the children with strangers.

Within the family unit, the grandparents watched over children between the ages four to eleven. Their role was to educate and discipline the little children in a patient loving way. The children grew up to be happy gentle people. It was good for the grandparents and the children and the parents.

Teens and young adults accompanied older uncles and aunts to be trained by them in special work.

Children were taught from the time they could learn. Skills such as fishing, hunting, tanning hides and making baskets were taught with great patience. By the time the child was grown, he or she already had what they needed to take full part in the community.

Harshness was not used in teaching children. Learning was always made very easy at first then it gradually became harder, but only as much the child could do well at. There was no such thing as failure. Teaching them through **success** opened up the child at a very young age to being good at things. They were then ready to do harder things later, without fear of failing.

Children found out what not to do through a sense of learning to be responsible to their family teachers. It is a syilx law to teach that each person is responsible to the rest of the people, to be a healthy part of the whole family and community. Adults are responsible to teach about this at an early age by showing very clearly how our actions are always tied to others, and how some actions disappoint and hurt their teachers and their family; the people they love most.

By the time the child became an adult, he knew how to respect others and how to live within the family unit, the extended family, the community and the whole nation and the land. This is good governance and the laws of the syilx as a people.

There was no such thing as an orphan, because the whole family, not only the direct parents was responsible to teach, love and provide for children. Each person then has a right, even when unborn, to family, to teachings and to security and love. No one can be left out. This is good governance because all syilx are important and must be cared for.

One of the most outstanding laws of the syilx is to learn to live and work in harmony with everyone and share with everyone in the community. We were taught in the cəpcaptíkʷɬ story of turtle that we must not think only of ourselves as individuals. We were taught that having more than others has to do with power and control of others. We are taught that it is wrong to have more things while others go without **in your community or family**. Wealth is to be enjoyed by all in times of plenty, and hardship is to be faced by all in bad times. The people stay strong together that way and it is good governance.

Another law was that every person shared equally in the work and its benefits. The highest form of good government is one in which all the members are healthy, housed and protected. In such a society, there is no need for **enforcement** laws because people don't steal from each other. Real self-government means all the people govern themselves without enforcement.

Good government, to the syilx, means that we carry the laws inside us. It means that we know how to act and live right without having someone force us. The syilx people were masters at civilization in that way. We know that those who do not know these simple laws are savage, barbaric and uncivilized. We call such people "wildmen" because they are lawless.

The syilx had no schools, jails, judges or police. No person ever went hungry while they were part of a village. Rape or child abuse was unknown. People were strong and lived to be old and were free all their lives. Gathering food and everyday work was shared and there was lots of time to spend on creative and interesting things. The syilx were great story tellers, artists, crafters, thinkers, singers, and musicians. They were the best of natural scientists and doctors. They excelled at sports and were extensive travellers. Our history shows all of this.

If the poor landless people from Europe had not been so busy fencing off properties for their governments, they might have learned a great deal from the syilx. We might not be living in the middle of the savageness we see every day in the news and on the streets everywhere. Perhaps if landless poor people in Canada would look at the unjustness which the legal system really protects, the way we see it, we would not be in the mess we are today. Perhaps they would know that they too have **human** rights, to live in health on the land in peace.

2

MANIFEST DESTINY

The early history of the French and the English in Canada and their relations with the original peoples of this land is important to the decisions we face as xatmaʔsqílxʷ, now. The legal ties which the provinces, the Federal Government, Britain, the USA must live up to are rooted in the history of early settlement. The history is best looked at as to what those relationships are, rather than simply the past, because those relationships became Countries. The relationships are what allowed the settlers to organize governments here and are the inherited rights of **everyone** here.

The East coast of North America's occupation by Britain began in 1497 when John Cabot (an Italian hired by England) landed in Newfoundland and huge numbers of codfish were seen. Fishing ships from England, France, Portugal and Spain began to fish off Newfoundland and south down the east coast to Cape Cod.

English fishing fleets began to settle the coastline lands to "dry" fish after having learned this method from the Aboriginal people. The English merchants began to trade with them for furs and foodstuffs.

More than a century later, the English set up settlements along what is now the eastern United States. These settlements depended on good relations with the aboriginal people, the five nations of the Iroquois Confederacy, in order to set up colonies for trade purposes. Good relations with Britain was based upon mutual respect and good trade practice. The British trader/settlers depended on the Iroquois for many things such as corn, beans and squash and traded for things the Iroquois wanted.

The Iroquois already had a great government of five United Nations working together peacefully before the Europeans got to North America. The Confederacy of five Nations included the Mohawks, the Oniedas, the Cayugas, the Senecas and the Onandagas. Each is a separate nation which agreed to cooperate and live separate customs and trade in peace and help to protect each other. Together they were called the Haudenosaunee (Iroquois) and all followed the great law of peace. They were a powerful government when the Europeans met them.

In 1535 Jacques Cartier of France reached Hochelaga (now Montreal) in the Gulf of Saint Lawrence and set up fur trade among the aboriginal people of that area. By the end of that century fur trade was in place. France set up its first colony called Port Royal in Western Nova Scotia, in what became known as Acadia, in 1605 for the purpose of cod fishing and fur trade. It was not such a money making colony. In the years following, control went back and forth between the English and French through both war and peaceful actions. Because of this the settler Acadians were unwilling to take sides when wars broke out between the French and English.

Samuel de Champlain of France founded the trade colony of Quebec in 1608. It became known as Canada and slowly spread out up the Saint Lawrence River. Champlain was friendly with the aboriginal people in that area to trade for furs. He chose to befriend the Algonquins and the Huron Confederacy who were fighting at the time with the Iroquois confederacy.

In 1609 Champlain went inland just to hunt Mohawks to prove his friendship with the Algonquins and Hurons. At what is now called Lake Champlain, he shot two chiefs of the Iroquois. The French became the enemy of the Iroquois.

Champlain urged his men to live with the aboriginal people he had befriended of that area. They became good woodsmen and trappers and travelled and traded freely as friends of the Algonquins and the Huron Confederacy and were openly hostile to the Iroquois. In the next fifty years the French in Canada intermarried into those Nations. They began to become more a part of the nations into which they had intermarried.

After Champlain was gone, a new policy forbade Frenchmen from living with the natives and trading without licences which were hard to get. Many of these Frenchmen escaped the colony, to continue to live with and marry into the Aboriginal Nations and were no longer loyal to France. The descendants of these "couriers de bois" are Metis. Rather than trade their furs with Quebec, they traded their furs with Albany (now in New York State) a trade post on the Hudson River.

Albany had been set up in 1609 by Henry Hudson working for the Dutch. It was set up as a Dutch trade post and was turned over to the British in 1664 and named New York.

Two of these "courier de bois" men, who were punished because of exploring into Cree territory north of Lake Superior, left the French Colony in disgust and offered their service to the English. Their knowledge with natives and the woods in the territory and the amount of furs they brought out was seen as valuable to the English. Because of the trade relations with the "courier de bois", the Hudson's Bay Company was chartered (given a licence by Britain for trade only) in 1670. All lands which could be reached from the Hudson's Bay Strait were licensed to them for that purpose and became known as Rupert's land.

The English ring of trade posts around the Hudson's Bay became a point from which to trade with the Cree and other nations. From then on the "courier de bois" and their relationships with the aboriginal people were extremely important in guiding the English westward to establish more fur trade posts.

In 1663 the King of France made Canada into a Royal Colony and pushed men and women to move there from France because the population of the colony of Quebec had become so small. Smaller than the English Colonies. In 1669 an edict (a legal paper) was passed to increase the population. Frenchwomen were brought to keep the men from escaping and making aboriginal families. Eligible men had to be married within 15 days of the ships of girls arriving or they would not be allowed to do fur trading. Girls had to be married by age 16 and boys by age 20 or they faced a fine. Those who did were rewarded with a royal gift of twenty liveres each. The population grew quickly and spread out.

In 1671 the French staged a ceremony attended by many tribes and the entire region from Sault St. Marie to the Pacific was announced to be taken in the name of the King of France. More trade posts were set up in the years following, until the French began to set up posts in territory claimed by the Hudson's Bay company.

Fighting between the French and the Iroquois grew as a result of the French invasions into trade territories of the Iroquois around Lake Superior. After some Iroquois raids on French posts, in 1666, the French attacked the Iroquois twice in what is now New York State across the Saint Lawrence River. Four Mohawk villages and all their vast winter supply of foods were destroyed. The Iroquois, who were already fighting with the Illinois Indians, called for a truce in 1667 with the French. For the next eighteen years the fighting between the Iroquois and the French did stop as the Iroquois kept their word.

The French at the same time had begun making friends with the Illinois Indians because they wanted to gain fur trade in the Mississippi valley. The French broke the truce with the Iroquois. They decided to back up the Illinois as a way to get control over their trade. They also wanted their help to stop the Iroquois in their new fur trade relations with the northern Algonquins, who had an easy route to the English Hudson's Bay trade posts in the north.

The French became afraid of losing control over fur trade with the friends they had. The Iroquois were strongly taking control over fur trade in the whole region and their trade went to the English who supplied them with guns. Other English goods were cheaper and other natives were beginning to trade with them as well. The French began to raid Iroquois villages again. The Iroquois fought back over the next years.

The Iroquois became strong allies with the English with whom they had always cooperated and traded in peace. The alliance between the English and the Iroquois Confederacy was sealed at a Grand council at Albany in 1684. Lord Howard Essingham, Governor General of Virginia, spoke of a new chain of covenant "strong and lasting even to the word's end".

The Iroquois became a protection and a battle zone between the French and the English Colonies. The French, helped by their Algonquian allies, sent hit-and-run raiding parties into New England, New York, Schenectedy and Salmon Falls to scalp, torture and burn English people in their homes. Many Iroquois died protecting the alliance with the English and with it their own nations' lands.

By 1700 the Iroquois had suffered losses from war and disease. Their numbers fell and by the 1690's, huge adoptions of other Iroquoians and Hurons was necessary. However, many of the adopted Iroquoians and their relatives converted to the Catholic religion and some of them were persuaded to settle on reserves granted by France, near Montreal. This also divided and weakened the Iroquois confederacy.

The French and the English agreed to a truce with each other in 1689. Soon after the Iroquois decided to meet with the French. In 1701 the Iroquois held a council with the French in Montreal and agreed to make peace with them and the thirteen western tribes who were friendly with the French. That hard won peace didn't last long, however, as the English and French began fighting again later that same year.

The French colony grew bigger to the west and north. Fighting broke out between the English and French trade posts over those next years. Under the Treaty of Utrecht in 1713, the Hudson's Bay trade region was awarded to the British in a treaty between France and Britain to settle war debts in Europe between France and Britain. This took place even though the French in Canada and its allies had defeated the English posts at Hudson's Bay. The French handed over all its claims to Newfoundland, any claims on the Hudson's Bay and **formally** recognized the British relationship with the Iroquois Confederacy.

France also handed over control of Nova Scotia to the English. This action enraged the Micmacs as English settlers began to intrude on their lands, without the yearly French "gift giving" practice of rent for the use of their lands. The Micmacs got weapons and ammunition from the French naval base which remained at Louisburg (Cape Breton Island). For almost fifty years the Micmacs fought and resisted the English with the urging of the French Acadians who had lived side by side with and intermarried with the Micmacs.

In 1749 the Micmacs declared war on the English. The English Governor then issued a proclamation to "annoy, distress, take or destroy the Savages community called the Micmacs, wherever they are found." The English paid for Indian scalps brought in. From 1713 to 1760 the Micmacs captured eighty English trading and fishing boats. The Micmacs eventually stopped their attacks after the English captured Acadian military garrisons when the Acadians refused to swear oaths of allegiance to Britain.

On the Island of Newfoundland, the Beothuk suffered greatly from the English and other European settlers. Without stop, they were killed and raided in their camps and pushed from their beaches and fisheries on the rivers. The Beothuk became starved and weakened because the sea was their only food source. They tried to fight off the settlers over the next hundred years. The settlers were ruthless in their killing off of as many Beothuks as possible. Because the Beothuks were not in a location where the English or the French could use them for fighting each other, they were never armed and were killed off. Their numbers dropped to extinction. In 1829 the last known Beothuk died. She was a servant in the household of an English Justice of the Peace. She was released to record the history of her people when she got sick with TB.

The French settlements along the Saint Lawrence River grew over those years and the ties to France became less important. Over the next generations the colonists began to think of themselves as "Canadien" rather than French people away from home. A population of country farmers (habitants) grew quickly. With it came a new lifestyle no longer dependant on France and the fur trade centres such as Quebec, Mount Royal, Montreal and Ottawa. The "Canadiens" were not easy to force into joining the wars.

The "Canadiens" strengthened their military positions along Lakes Ontario and Champlain and began to war with the Fox Nation along Lake Michigan. Their strength was their allies from that area. A system of diplomatic gift giving, yearly, of supplies like ammunition and guns, kept their allies loyal. Their aboriginal allies acknowledged these presents as an annual form of rent for the use of the land on which the French forts stood and as a fee for the right to travel across their territory. The aboriginal allies stayed in control over their lands and limited French rule to the forts.

In 1744 war broke out in Europe between England and France. In 1745 the English Colonies raised a force and waged war on the French naval base of Louisburg on the Eastern tip of Cape Breton in Acadia (Nova Scotia). The English captured

Louisburg. They eventually deported the Acadians from Nova Scotia because of their resistance along with the Micmac against the English. The English decided to disperse them among the Colonies where most of them died in poverty and slavery. Some of them made it to Quebec and some to the two small islands off Newfoundland that still belonged to France. Some twenty-five hundred Acadians and Metis Acadians made it to the swamplands of Louisiana. Their descendants are now known as the Cajun and number around one million.

With the fall of Louisburg, things grew worse for the French over the next ten years. Without Louisburg as a naval supply base, the British had open season on French supply ships. Without the supply of guns and ammunition from the French to their allies, the Great Lakes allies were no longer friendly. In 1747 anger between the Wyandot and the Algonquins began to grow toward the French.

In 1754 the Governor of Virginia got orders to wipe out the French rule on the Saint Lawrence. A small troop under George Washington, together with a troop of Iroquois allies, were sent to expel the French. A force of five hundred Canadiens, French troops and Allies attacked and defeated Washington's troops. This victory brought the allies of the French back into line.

Full war broke out between the French in Canada and the English Colonies. From 1755 for the next two years the French and their allies gained the upper hand by fighting like their allies, in hit-and-run raids and in the forest as guerillas. The Canadien/Indian war parties caused terror on all the English colonies and touched off slave uprisings.

The Wars between 1755-1763 were called the French and Indian Wars. French troops had large numbers of Aboriginal Allies fighting for them. The English Colonists, as well, had Iroquois troops fighting with them. The English Colonists brought in British troops to help in the war and eventually gained the upper hand because the French were much fewer in numbers even with their allies.

In 1759 the English beat the French on the Plains of Abraham near the most important stronghold of Quebec. In 1760 the French gave up and New France passed into British hands. The terms of surrender under which the French in Canada agreed to come under British rule allowed for their freedom to continue their customs, practice their Catholic religion and to keep their property.

In the years following the French surrender, the Great Lakes allies of the French became more and more angry at the British and the English Colonists land-grabbing. Unlike the French, the English made one-time payment treaties and land purchases around the colonies on the east coast. The French had made yearly payments and acknowledged the rule of the allies in their own territories. The English thought that by defeating the French it got control and ownership of the lands in which the French traded and had allies. They would not make yearly rental payments for use of aboriginal territories.

In 1763, Chief Pontiac of the Ottawa organized a large Aboriginal Nations Allied Forces to oppose the British. They captured every British fort west of the Niagara except Detroit. However, this totally halted fur trade in the area. As their supplies of ammunition began to run out, Pontiac's Allied Forces made hasty moves to trade for some from wherever they could, even at enemy English forts. The cost was much greater than the high prices they were forced to pay.

As a way to stop resistance, the English, that fall, at Fort Pitt (Pittsburg), gave the Indians a "present" of two blankets and a handkerchief from the fort's smallpox ward. The results were an epidemic, and slowly Pontiac's confederacy began to weaken. Although the resistance was weakened, the English had to fight continuously over the next year to keep their trade routes open.

The resistance and its results on the settlements west of Niagara, had an effect on the fur trade and the economy of Britain. The British Board of Trade and Plantations in London had already began plans to appease the Aboriginal Nations. Pontiac's courageous revolt made it clear that the plans needed to be carried out quickly.

The **Royal Proclamation** of King George III was issued in 1763 at the urging of the British Board of Trade. The Royal Proclamation was the legal tool by which the old English colonies and the new Colony of Canada were to make trade relations with Aboriginal Nations in trade territories newly under British Authority. It set out the boundaries and their duties in getting access to the west for settlements and trade.

The Proclamation set aside a huge reserve west of the Allegheny mountains for those with whom the Colonies were allied and who were under their protection. The main intent of the Proclamation was to **preserve** the west as an Indian territory and keep it for sole trade access by Britain's trade merchants. The need to end fighting was a priority. This program of controlled use was to be managed **totally** from **Britain.** There **was to be no** interference by the old or new colonies who had their own merchant companies and were beginning to resist British rule. As well, it would end any question with the Aboriginal Nations of France's previous claims to the lands and trade relations.

In the interest of **peaceful trade and settlement**, in the Proclamation, Britain agreed it had **no right to colonize** without first buying lands occupied by Aboriginal owners. It proclaimed that **consent** must be obtained in an agreement (treaty) of **any** of the Aboriginal Nations and Tribes west of the heads of all the rivers which flowed into the Atlantic.

All lands west of the Canadian Shield were included in that **legal guarantee**. Land grants and surveying was forbidden, and together with trade relations were to be managed directly by Britain. The recognition of Aboriginal ownership and the right to **retain ownership** unless lands were properly **ceded** to the British Crown, were the grounds upon which **peace** was finally made with the Aboriginal Peoples. By this Proclamation **The Crown** obliged itself legally to a relationship of recognition of **aboriginal** ownership of **all** lands west of the colonies and set legal precedent for all aboriginal lands upon which the Crown had established a relationship.

After the surrender of the French in Canada to Britain, the Quebec Act in 1774 **confirmed** what the terms of surrender outlined and insured. Its main intent was to get the friendship of the new "French Canadien" subjects tied to Britain. The Quebec Act set out what became officially known as the "province" of Quebec and allocated the region between the Ohio and the Mississippi rivers where some French had settled for further expansion. This part of the Quebec Act was also a clever measure to stop merchants from the old English Colonies from moving westward and getting trade relations with the Aboriginal Nations and Tribes. Although it kept Quebec quiet and the British merchants of Halifax and Nova Scotia, happy, the Quebec Act became the centre of the American revolution.

The Quebec Act was the spark which ignited the anger of the old colonies who no longer felt they were a part of Britain. Growing population and plenty of foods and goods from plantations and slave trade and industry led to a spread outward of settlers from the colonies. The question of what the colonies needed from the British motherland had become a serious concern.

Britain's control over merchant trade on land and sea and laying of heavy taxes on the colonies to pay for the war effort, enraged the colonies. The colonists pushed to break ties with Britain and the growing idea of self-rule grew stronger in resistance to the Quebec Act. The colonists also saw how the Quebec Act protected the Imperial trade interests of Britain to the west. In 1775 the old colonists invaded Canada without real serious damage, however the "American" revolution became official and the declared independence from Britain in 1776 followed.

In 1783 the Treaty of Paris ended the struggle between Britain and the Americans. In the treaty the British recognized American independence and protection was given to British Empire loyalists wishing to leave the colonies. The Treaty recognized a clear boundary between Canada and America on land and on the North Atlantic.

However, in the treaty, the Americans refused to define any boundaries separating the territory of the United States from the lands of the Aboriginal Nations and Tribes. In the following twenty years, continued bickering over those boundaries and Britain's interference of American trade in Europe led to more disagreements. This and two more serious causes later led to another outbreak of war.

What was called the "Indian problem" was a serious factor. During the war of Independence the British had taken great care to keep the friendship of their Aboriginal Allies and the "French Canadien" allies by "presents" and high payment for furs. After the war several thousand Iroquoian loyalists moved to Upper Canada. These were mostly Mohawk, Cayuga and Onandaga who had fought for Britain. The British moved quickly to help them settle on reserves of their choosing.

In the years after 1783 and Treaty of Paris, the British supported the Aboriginal Nations claims in every dispute with American settlers, in the territories west beyond the Alleghenies. The Americans said that British agents supplied the Aboriginal Nations with weapons and urged them to attack the frontier American settlements. The Americans saw a way to settle the "Indian problem" by seizing their lands and also forcing the British to give up their forts in the upper Mississippi Valley. It was the biggest reason in the decision to go to war again. The Americans wished to drive Britain from the whole of North America and carry out what it had failed to do in 1775. It's leaders called this an effort to "free" Upper and Lower Canada.

In 1812, war was declared by the United States of America. An army of two thousand invading Canada, from Detroit was defeated by a small troop of English loyalists and five hundred Aboriginal Allies. The English capture of Detroit, Fort Michilimackinac and Frenchtown on Lake Erie, again made strong the Indian alliance with them. They fought in great numbers alongside the British. The Americans accused the English of allowing the "Indians" to kill the captured American wounded. The English lost the battle for the Forts across Lake Erie. The Americans killed Chief Techumseh who had led the allies. The Americans then gained control of the Michigan territory.

York (Toronto), the capital of Upper Canada was also assaulted. At Fort George, a tiny troop of fifty Canadians and a similar sized band of Aboriginal Allied Forces fooled the Americans into surrendering. The Americans were slowly driven south over the next two years as British forces arrived from England. In 1814 the British navy gained control of the whole East Coast to Maine and had captured Washington, the capital of the United States. After suffering an attack on Baltimore, the fighting on the east coast stopped.

In 1814 the Treaty of Ghent was signed between Britain and the United States of America. It agreed **on a return** to the way things were before the war, rather than to give Maine and other posts captured in the United States over to Britain. The Treaty of Ghent carried forward **formally** the principle of the Jay's Treaty (Treaty of amnesty and Commerce 1794) which had been put in place for trade and commerce between Canada and the United States. The Treaty of Ghent bound **both** countries to make peace with the Aboriginal Nations they traded with and abide by the Jay's Treaty.

In the years to follow, one of the outcomes of the French fur trade outposts in the interior along the Great Lakes had been the rise of a large population of Metis. The descendants of the Frenchmen, who had married into aboriginal families, were at the front of the move westward as guides and traders. Their settlements expanded from the Upper Great Lakes to the Red River Valley and south through the plains to the Arkansas River. At the place where the Red and the Assiniboine Rivers meet, (now Winnipeg), the Metis had made large permanent farming settlements.

The Hudson's Bay Company had set up a farming colony of mostly Scottish farmers who had been removed from their own lands and created the District of Assiniboia. The Hudson's Bay rival, the North West Company, became angry because this threatened their supplies to interior posts. Many Metis were intermarried with the North West Company traders and were living at the North West posts. The North Westers pushed the Metis into an uprising against the Selkirk Colony. A battle at Qu'Appelle led by the Metis drove out the Selkirk colony. The victory united the Metis into taking a stand as a nation and to claim their land rights through their Cree mothers.

The Metis organized large powerful armed units for annual trapping and the hunting of buffalo. They were allied with the Crees with whom they had blood ties. As a result there was no resistance to hunt, trap or settle on lands of the Cree. They began to test the control of the Hudson's Bay company to sell furs and buffalo meat to colonists. From the 1850's the Metis colony grew and spread out. They began to make many long trips to St. Paul in the United States to sell furs and to buy supplies. By the 1860's they were powerful and wealthy from farming and trading. The Hudson's Bay Company lost control.

The Civil War which had taken place in the meantime in the United States had created an anti-British feeling against Canada. There was a growing belief in Canada that if **British** North America was to survive, it was necessary to join into one federated unit. Another good reason for unity was to make trade stronger between the British provinces rather than south into the United States.

With fear of American takeover as the main force, in 1867, the British North America Act was passed by Britain's Parliament allowing the Canadians to make policy to govern themselves as a unit. A central federal power over the provinces was the result, with the ties of that central power to Britain's parliament.

The agreements which Britain had made with the Aboriginal Peoples were given protection in section 91-24 of the British North America Act. The Federal Government was assigned a duty to watch over the Crown's relationship with "Indians" and "Indian" lands. The word "Indian", a generic racist term, which Canada had adopted from the American's policy of non-recognition of Aboriginal Nations was used in the wording, instead of the words Aboriginal Nations and Tribes as had been set out in the Royal Proclamation. The term implies that "Indians" are one large group without separate rights as Nations or Tribes and therefore are all subject to one policy.

In 1869 the Hudson's Bay Company agreed to turn over its territorial trade rights to Britain to allow the region to become a colony. The French speaking Metis refused to accept the control of an English governor with good reason. It was their relationship to the Cree that had allowed trade and peaceful settlement in that territory. They set up a government with Louis Riel as their leader.

The threatened loss of their lands and the end of trade into the United States was an assault on the rights that they had clearly won through their efforts. Riel's Government set up a road block along the Red River highway south of Fort Garry (Winnipeg). Riel's government did not allow the new British Governor to enter their lands. They seized Fort Garry. Riel called for delegates from the English-speaking population to join with the French Metis in a convention that would represent the whole colony. The convention agreed to a list of rights which had to be guaranteed to them all. Riel worked to convince Britain and Ottawa to recognize their provisional government.

An agreement was reached and the terms of transfer of powers to the new governor was granted. Riel had won the Metis self-rule he thought could protect his people. However the terms of agreement did not give amnesty (release from legal blame) to him or his followers. Riel's government's execution of Thomas Scott, a rebellious Orangeman from Ontario who had worked against Riel, sparked racial bitterness in Ottawa toward the French Catholic Metis.

Under that excuse, Canada sent a British and Canadian military force in August 1870 to the Red River. Force was continued although Riel was satisfied with the agreement reached and the settlement was quiet when reached by the Ontario Militia. The violence and the arrogance the Ontario militia exercised toward Riel's people, in which great losses were suffered was extreme and had no basis except racism. To save his life, Riel fled into exile in the United States. He lived and traded among the many Metis in Minnesota and the Dakota's and Montana.

In May of 1870 the Manitoba Act was passed granting provincial government status. It granted respect for existing customs and property rights, adequate finances and equality of French and English as official languages. The Manitoba act transferred the District of Assiniboia into the new province. The remainder of the West was to be administered as the Northwest territories under an appointed governor and council.

An amendment to the British North America Act was passed by Britain in 1871 confirming the Manitoba Act and the legislation on the Northwest Territories. The amendment also gave the Dominion of Canada the right to create new provinces and decide their terms of entry.

Fifteen years later the Metis and their Cree allies, Poundmaker and Big Bear, were in open rebellion against Canada again. In open disrespect of the terms of the Manitoba Act, there was open taking of Cree and Metis lands and laws passed against the custom of harvesting buffalo by any Metis. Louis Riel was sent for. He asked for the help of some of his American friends and returned. War broke out.

The rebellion ended in the defeat of Riel. The government allowed the killing of Louis Riel for the death of Thomas Scott who Riel had sentenced to death for rebellion under his provisional government fifteen years earlier. It caused great argument and almost split Canada. The Red River was then thrown open to settlers without regard for the Metis peoples' rights guaranteed in the terms of the Manitoba Act.

Treaties surrendering lands to the Crown in the Great Plains began in 1871. The treaties surrendered much of the fertile lands of the plains west to the Rockies, opening it up for legal settlement by Canada in return for on-going yearly benefits in good trade value of the time. The Aboriginal Peoples **reserved lands** for their exclusive use. Treaties allowed peaceful side-by-side life next to settlers. The treaties agree to permanent peaceful land-use extended to Great Britain, in return for benefits, which must be met until Britain or the Treaty Nations changed that.

The Federal Government was given the responsibility to make policy to watch over the Canadian people in their actions in the Crown's duty to Aboriginal Nations and their lands. This duty is clearly set out in the treaties and in the Royal Proclamation provisions where no treaties existed. That duty comes from the French and Indian wars and the American Revolution and Britain's relations with its Aboriginal Allies which allowed it an advantage.

By its policies, Canada interpreted the duty to the "Indians" in the Indian Act, to mean that the Federal Government was given **jurisdiction** over "Indians" as one generic group. It therefore interprets that to mean it has **jurisdiction** over their lands.

The British North America Act was an act to allow settlers to govern themselves on lands "properly ceded and surrendered" to the Crown. Canada had no powers to have jurisdiction on lands **not ceded** and **not surrendered**, which all Aboriginal Nations lands, treatied or untreatied are. The aboriginal owners have jurisdiction. No legal rule established otherwise.

The BNA Act could not somehow automatically give reserved lands or Aboriginal Peoples on them, to the newly organized group of British subjects in North America. To do so would have made Canada a legal power greater than the Crown in the signing of treaties under the Royal Proclamation. Canada was only an act of Britain's parliament.

Oral treaty Agreements were made by Governor Douglas for **Britain** within the policy of the Royal Proclamation, in the interior of British Columbia, before the British North America Act was passed. The duty to continue to "treat with" the aboriginal people was stated in the legal way that the Colony of B.C. joined Canada in 1871.

Governor Douglas bound the government to a process by practise and a clearly demonstrated intent to practise. He did this by setting a clear precedent of compliance with the Royal Proclamation, in having made actual treaties which ceded lands clearly defined in the wording of the Proclamation as lands:

"Lying to the Westward of the source of the Rivers which fall into the Atlantic from the West and North West, or upon any lands whatever, which not having been ceded to or purchased by Us as aforesaid, are reserved to the said Indians, or any of them ..... And .... strictly forbid our Subjects from making purchase or Settlements whatever, or taking possession of any of the Lands above without our especial leave and licence for that Purpose first obtained. And, we...strictly ..require all Persons ...who have willfully or inadvertantly seated them selves upon ....lands which, not having been ceded to or purchased by us, are still reserved to the said Indians as aforesaid, forthwith to remove themselves from such settlements....If at any time any of the Said Indians should be inclined to dispose of the said lands, the same shall be purchased only for Us, in our Name, at some public Meeting or Assembly of the said Indians, to be held for that Purpose by the Governor or Commander in Chief of our colony...; and in case they(the lands) shall lie within the limits of any Proprietary Government, they shall be purchased only for the use and in the name of such Proprietaries, conformable to such Directions and Instructions as We or they shall give for that Purpose."

BRITISH COLUMBIA'S LIE

Large cuts were made on the original reserves which had been agreed to with Douglas in the interior of B.C. before Confederation. The cuts were not made known and certainly not agreed to by the Interior Aboriginal Nations, including the Okanagan. Large claims to the best farm lands in the Interior were made by people who were in government and employed by government. Direct **conflicts of interest** and lies were the ways by which the colonists took those lands.

In 1849, Vancouver Island was granted a charter to become a Colony to allow settlement. It had been changed from being a Hudson's Bay license allowing trade with the Aboriginal People. During those years, Governor Douglas signed fourteen treaties on Vancouver Island.

In 1858 with the discovery of gold on the Fraser River, a new colony on the mainland was claimed for Britain, by Governor Douglas. In 1859 the new colony was officially given the name British Columbia and was joined with Vancouver Island into one colony. Governor Douglas negotiated peace agreements **and reservations** with the Okanagans and other interior Indians from then until he retired.

In 1864 Governor Douglas retired and was replaced by Governor Seymour who was not strong in understanding the need for peaceful agreement with the Indians. In 1865, Joseph Trutch became the British Columbia Commissioner of Lands and Works and began to take control of Indian Policy through half truths under the weak Governor Seymour.

In clearly recorded racist intent, Trutch would not continue with the reserve policy which Governor Douglas had bound the government to. Trutch, assisted by Judge Hanes, in the years between 1865 and the joining of Canada's Confederation in 1871, severely cut down all the reserves which had been agreed to by the Aboriginal Nations with Governor Douglas. He did this without getting agreement from the Aboriginal Peoples as was Britain's proclaimed will. It was also against Governor Douglas's orders to the Vancouver Island House of Assembly, not to reduce the reserves he had agreed to. Trutch had no power to override the Crown's long proclaimed will for peaceful surrendering of lands to it.

Trutch's comments from Paper's related to B.C. PRE 1871

"The Indians really have no right to the lands they claim, nor are they of any actual value or utility to them...

It seems to me, therefore, both just and politic that they should be confirmed in the possession of such extents of land only as are sufficient for their probable requirement for purposes of cultivation and pasturage, and that the remainder of the land now shut up in these reserves should be thrown open to pre-emption."

Regardless of how Trutch acted on paper at that stage, the Crown Colony of British Columbia was already **legally** bound by the action taken by Governor Douglas on behalf of Britain. It **demonstrated intent** for due process. Douglas was empowered by Britain's parliament as Governor to make agreements, with the consent of the Aboriginal Peoples themselves.

In 1871 B.C. was allowed to join the Confederation of provinces into the British Dominion of Canada. The British Crown Colony approved entry by agreeing to terms that had to be met by Canada. Canada agreed to the terms set out by the Colony of British Columbia.

ARTICLE 13

The terms for treaty making were that Canada was to be as liberal as B.C. was before B.C. entered Confederation. This article **guarantees** agreements made by Governor Douglas. Under treaty making rules, the Douglas reserves were the only ones legally **consented** to by the Interior Nations. Clearly, Governor Douglas established a liberal policy in the Interior in making reserves through mutual agreement with Interior Chiefs.

Article 13 is a clear agreement that must be **met as a federal** responsibility to the Crown. The responsibility is **removed** fully from the provincial government from that point onward.

Clearly, the paper "reserves" enacted by Trutch, without surrender by treaty, required by British policy were not within legal policy. The Federal Government's responsibility was to complete due process as liberally as Governor Douglas had practised. In fact Governor Douglas outlined that policy and obligation to the Dominion government in 1874 when the first Reserve Commission was being established to question British Columbia's actions.

In the years immediately following Confederation, British Columbia chose to ignore the duty the Federal Government had in settling with the Aboriginal Peoples by proper treaties. Trutch defended his racist policy with half truths. Joseph Trutch was named the first lieutenant-governor of the new province.

The province pretended that the constitutional **right to make rules** (jurisdiction) about lands and resources, was an automatic giving of lands and resources to the province. The law is clear. For Canada, it can only be treaties which legally give lands over to the Crown. At the time of the colonies, lands were surrendered to Britain by treaty. After Confederation treaties still surrendered lands over to Britain because Canada was a Dominion of the Crown (owned by).

The lands are surrendered to Britain and then they pass into Canada's jurisdiction (the right to regulate) under the British North America Act. Neither Canada nor the provinces **automatically** owned or own lands, before or after Confederation. The BNA Act only grants the right to **occupy** and to **regulate** that use and occupation. Britain was the legal owner of Dominion lands surrendered to it.

The first step would have been to recognize agreements made with Governor Douglas. It was the legal duty of the Federal Government to put in place as was dictated by article 13. Where no agreements were made, then the same "liberal" policy must be applied by the Federal Government as was applied by Douglas.

This is strongly confirmed by **due process** carried out by the Federal Government right after Confederation in the rest of Canada. A clear policy of recognizing Aboriginal Peoples' rights and title to lands was shown in the way which lands were ceded to Britain in the signing of the numbered treaties in the prairies during the very same years of Trutch's term as lieutenant governor.

In the years right after Confederation, Trutch continued to lie about B.C. Government policy towards Indians and reserves as the argument grew between the province and Canada. The argument centred around the province not wanting to let go of any lands it said it already owned. It was made worse by the Federal Government not understanding clearly the situation in B.C. and not having a clear way to enforce its responsibility to the Crown and the Indians.

In 1874 Joseph Trutch retired as Lieutenant Governor. Two months later the Governor General of Canada, Earl Dufferin, criticized the B.C. Provincial policy for not doing its duty to "recognize what is known as Indian title... in British Columbia..." He pointed out that "the Provincial Government has always **assumed** that the fee simple as well as sovereignty over the land resided in the Queen". In other words he said that the B.C. Government operated through a false belief that the Crown somehow already owned the title and rights to B.C. lands although it didn't.

David Mills, Minister of the Department of the Interior, the following year said that at the time of Confederation, federal authorities were not informed that treaties had not been made with the Indians of B.C. for the surrender of their territory. He said that the Dominion had the **legal right** to interfere and prevent the Provincial

Government from dealing with any public land that had Indian title which had not been extinguished. He mentions, however, that as long as the Indians remained content, the Federal Government didn't want to raise the question of Indian title.

It is clear that there is an **admitted** looming legal question open as to the Federal Government's breach of trust to the Crown and to the Indians of B.C. It did **not** fulfil article 13 to which it had agreed and it did **not** carry out what is required in the Royal Proclamation to properly get surrender of lands in B.C. as it had done elsewhere. No matter how B.C. chose or chooses to act, it is still the Federal Government that must legally act on its duty.

In 1873 the federal department of the Interior was created and an Indian Lands branch is set up within it. A board of commissioners was named to administer Indian Affairs in Manitoba, B.C. and the NorthWest Territories.

In 1876 the Federal Government disallowed a proposal for British Columbia to pass a B.C. Crown Lands Act, which would allow British Columbia to administer and sell crown lands. It was not allowed on the basis that the surrender of aboriginal title had not been obtained.

In 1876 the first Indian Act was passed without any input or agreement from any Indians. The Indian Act at the outset was designed as a tool to control the Indians in key areas, while partly being obedient to section 91.24 of the British North America Act.

LIES IN THE OKANAGAN

In the Okanagan, before Confederation, Sir James Douglas, Governor of B.C. for Britain, had made oral agreements with the High Okanagan Chief . He agreed that lands pointed out by village chiefs themselves would be protected from being bothered by the "Queen's children" forever.

In 1859, gold was discovered in Rock Creek and in the spring of 1860, James Douglas appointed William Cox as Gold Commissioner and sent him to Rock Creek to collect customs duties. Reports of gold discovery in Mission Creek (Pandosy Mission) and on the Similkameen were reported by Judge Haynes, Revenue Collector and Customs Officer. Other discoveries were reported in the Okanagan at Princeton, Fort Shepherd, the Kettle River tributaries, and on the upper Columbia as well as many small mines around it.

Unruly miners began to crowd into the territory to stake mines. After several serious fights between Okanagans and miners at Rock Creek it became clear that it was necessary for Douglas to come to an official peaceful agreement with the Okanagans to allow him to administer justice to the White intruders. There is a petition letter from Chilheetza to Douglas which asks him to do just that.

Writing from Rock Creek, William Cox, Assistant Commissioner of Lands, reported on a meeting he held with the Lakes Indians. The purpose of the meeting was to settle any disputes between the Indians and miners. At this time, the Lakes Indians were found to be living along the shores of the Arrow Lakes north of Washington territory. Cox noted that all the "Indians of this portion of the Colony believe (the boundary line) to be intended as a barrier against the approach of the Boston man (Americans)." The high Chief Gugoin (Gregoire) was away and the meeting was attended by two other chiefs, Mikichlore and Qui-qui-las-ket. (Cox correspondence 1861, Rock Creek)

Aa - hah - peo - Tsa (Blanket was scratched (by grizzly)). Mary Narcisse - Ashnola Mary, Died 1944, age 116. Article in a local newsletter states she was likely 130 years old when she died.

Photo, Provincial Archives.

The attitude of those who were directly interested in owning land in the Okanagan was racist toward the Indian ownership of lands. William Cox, Assistant Commissioner of Lands and Judge Haynes, Revenue Collector and Customs Officer and Joseph Trutch, Commissioner of Public Works, were each involved in the laying out of reserves during this period. They were to administer Colonial justice, as well.

From 1858 to 1862, Governor Douglas' policy was to make large reserves. This was clearly spelled out in 1861 when Douglas instructed the reserve surveyors to lay out reserves to the extent "as they may... be pointed out by the Natives themselves." (from letter to Dominion Government 1874) This was done for the Fraser Valley, the Fraser Canyon, the Lillooet, Ashcroft, Kamloops, and the Okanagan. All of these original Douglas reserves were large. They included hunting, fishing territory as well as farm and grazing lands.

Nearly all the farm and grazing lands at the North and South end of Okanagan Lake was reserved by the N'kamepelks and the Sn'pnktn Chiefs and down the entire west side of the lake to past Okanagan Falls. Osoyoos Reserve included all lands on the east bank of the Okanagan River from Vaseaux Creek to the U.S. border. (Douglas Correspondence, Young to Cox 14 Nov. 1862, B.C. Colonial Secretary, Outward Correspondence).

These events were witnessed by the Chiefs. They were recorded in formal letters to Douglas and formal stakes placed on the corners of the lands identified by the Okanagan Chiefs (Cox to Douglas, 17 June 1861, reference to the identification stakes).

Many elders in the Okanagan can recount the fact that runners were sent out with the government men to point out the corners of these reserves. Harriet (Chilheetza) Paul, daughter of Chief John Chilheetza, stated at an Okanagan Shuswap confederacy meeting in Kamloops in 1982, the importance of these "corner posts" which her grandfather had agreed to. The stakes are described as having a brass or copper plate with Royal Seal and numbers driven into the top of each one.

Besides pointing out large reserves themselves, Okanagans kept full hunting and fishing rights on all lands around their reserves. Okanagans kept access to the lands outside their reserves. They had grazing areas and plenty of water to develop their lands. (Douglas, 1874 outline to the Dominion Government on his B.C. reserve policy).

Governor Douglas' promise to was that this agreement was to be protected forever. The words used were " As long as the sun rises and the rivers flow and the imperial flag continues to fly over Britain." This mutual agreement with Governor Douglas is the only direct consultation any foreign government ever had with Okanagan Chiefs and people about their rights as original peoples on that land.

The words used by the Governor in his meeting with all the Southern Interior Chiefs at Boston Bar is public record. It is public record that Governor Douglas recognized the ownership rights of the original people by going to them to make an agreement. He asked for a peaceful agreement so there would be no wars with the settlers.

It is record that Governor Douglas received the maps of the reserves the village chiefs pointed out and staked by his workers with four corner posts. These maps record reserves in Penticton, Osoyoos, and Head of the Lake.

Since the Colony of British Columbia was broke and owed money to Britain, it could not buy lands for the "Queen's children" to live on, even though it had done so on Vancouver Island. It is public record that Douglas tried to get money for that purpose but didn't get it. For that reason no surrender treaties were made and **no lands were surrendered** to Britain in the mainland of B.C.

The Royal Proclamation dictated that lands must be properly paid for and surrendered. Without money, a joint-use agreement was the only thing that could be bargained for. Governor Douglas did that in the Okanagan by agreeing that the **village sites** of each Band would be reserved and given full protection from trespass while the Crown's "children" would have **access** to other lands. These oral agreements did **not** surrender the ownership or the resource rights to the lands outside the "reserved lands."

After Governor Douglas retired, from 1864 to Confederation, no attempt was made to inform the Okanagan People of changes in the Colony's attitude. Joseph Trutch, who was hired for lands and works by the new Governor Seymour, deliberately cut down the reserves, saying that savages had no use for land. He simply drew lines on paper and called them reserves. These "reserves" were not agreed to by anyone with ownership.

In the Okanagan, as elsewhere in B.C., in the years after Confederation, severe action was taken by the province against Indians who strayed out of the tiny lands shown, only on paper, as reserves. The Okanagans, weakened in numbers by a wave of smallpox in the 1860's, were unable to fight back. The result was anger as starvation became disease and caused widespread death.

The provincial authorities and settlers harassed Okanagan people for gathering food and hunting on lands that they had always used for that purpose. The tiny "reserves" they were expected to survive on could not feed them. Lands that somehow without agreement of any kind were said to no longer belong to the Okanagan.

The trust with which the Okanagans allowed the colonists to enter the Okanagan in peace, became a focus for outrage. The numbers of the settlers had grown big enough to bully and break their promises to a people weakened by starvation and disease but that did not make it right or legal.

The Okanagans decided to go to war to drive the liars out of their territory. It was a matter of survival at that point. In 1874 there was a flurry of messages sent to Ottawa reporting an Indian outbreak if measures were not taken to quickly correct the situation.

The Oblate priests who had set up a mission near Kelowna were trusted by many Chiefs of the Okanagan. In 1874, Grandidier, an Oblate priest at the mission, in a famous letter to the Victoria Standard News, pointed out the wrong doing. He pleaded on behalf of the Okanagan people, on government action to do right.

Excerpt of the Grandidier letter;

To the Editor of the Victoria Standard:
August 18, 1874

. . . When the Dominion Government took charge of the Indian tribes of British Columbia it was proposed to adopt the same policy towards them as towards their brothers of the other Provinces, and grant each family a large quantity of land. To this proposition the Local Government objected, and would not grant more than twenty (20) acres.

. . . Many of these reservations have been surveyed without their consent, and sometimes without having received notice of it, so that they could not expose their needs and their wishes. Their reservations have been repeatedly cut off smaller for the benefit of the whites, and the best and most useful part of them taken away till some tribes are corralled on a small piece of land . . ., or even have not an inch of ground, . . . The natives have protested against those spoilations, from the beginning. They have complained bitterly of that treatment, but they have not obtained any redress.

. . . The land was theirs and their forefathers before the whites came; that land has been wrenched from them in virtue of might, not right; not a cent has been given them to extinguish their title to the land. They have been left to struggle on the parcel of land allotted them without any encouragement, any help, any agricultural implements from any quarter, and, because they are forbearing and peacefully disposed, they are to be granted the minimum possible of land.

I appeal to every impartial mind, is that treatment according to Justice? And are not the natives justified in now claiming their rights? . . . Besides their lands were valuable to the Indians for hunting, and now the game is receding far away before the whites. It was valuable to them for their horses, and now their horses and cattle have no ground to feed upon, . . .

. . . They do not think that when a white man can pre–empt 320 acres and buy as much more, besides the facility of leasing more, that they are unreasonable in asking 80 acres of their own land per family; and in that they are supported by the example of the dominion Government's conduct towards the other Indians . . .

. . . If a white man can scarcely eke out a living with his 320 acres how can an Indian do it with 20? . .

. . . Besides, a good part of the reservation, with a few exceptions, is either overflooded in summer, or parched for want of water which cannot be brought there, covered with timber, or strewn with rocks, as any visitor may convince himself.

But if the Indians are persistently refused their demands, if redress from the proper authorities, their dissatisfaction will increase, meetings shall be held again, as it has been about their grievances, until they come to an understanding, the end of which I am afraid to foresee...

C.J. Grandidier

Between 1875 and 1877 the Okanagan Chiefs called a council of war with their allies, the Shuswaps and formed a confederacy. An Indian uprising was feared from Spallumcheen to Osoyoos.

Telegram exerpt from letter of Commission 1877

Fear of armed rebellion in the Interior necessitated immediate action and the Commission arrived in Kamloops in the Spring of 1877. They were impressed enough with the gravity of the situation to wire Ottawa: **"Indian situation very grave from Kamloops to American border - general dissatisfaction - outbreak possible."**

Pressure from the settlers forced the Governments to form a Royal Commission to settle the matter between the province and Canada and the Aboriginal Nations of B.C. The Commission consisted of a representative of the Federal Government (Alexander Anderson), a representative of the provincial government (Archibald McKinley) and one agreed to by both (Gilbert Malcolm Sproat). The Order-in-Council gave powers to the commission only to negotiate the **size** of reserves and **not to negotiate** the larger question of underlying title or rights.

Excerpt from David Mills, Minister of the Interior to the Commission

The Canadian Government were not disposed to raise the question of the general rights of the Indian population to the soil in British Columbia, so long as the Indians were contented. They would prefer not to do so now; but they cannot fail to perceive that there is great danger of an Indian war growing out of the land policy of the Provincial Government.

In order that the question may not be raised, and war avoided, it is of the utmost consequence that the Commissioners, in setting apart Reservations for Indians, should make them as ample as to avoid the necessity, if possible, of raising the question.

The first thing the Joint commission did was to meet with the Okanagan Shuswap Confederacy and make promises. It shows from their reports that they saw their job as doing whatever was necessary to quiet the group while settling the argument between the governments. The reports say that they thought their best strategy would be to divide the confederacy. This would be done by making large offers, individually, to the **smallest** bands of the confederacy.

Exerpt McKinley, Sproat, Anderson Commission reports, 1876-1878

We have the honour to annex copy of your telegram received at Savona's Ferry on the 23 inst., in reply to ours of the 13th inst., to the Honourable Minister of the Interior .... So far as our special duties are concerned, we are going on as usual and are personally well received everywhere by the Indians, among whom we go unarmed as their friends, and without any wish to be a show of force.

We hope that we have not been unsuccessful in calming to some extent the minds of those with whom we have had interviews and in gaining a portion of their confidence though we are sorry to say we cannot advise you of any great improvement in the situation of affairs, so far.... The Indians hold Councils frequently, and messengers pass to and fro.

We believe we have succeeded in withdrawing two tribes from the Shuswap Confederation, and if we can withdraw one or two more within the next fortnight, which may be possible, as the confidence of the Indians in our representations as to the justice and liberality of the governments increases, we may be able to advise that we see our way hopefully to some substantial progress in the work we have in hand....

Repeated attempts were made by the Chiefs to address the larger question. The commission quieted the Chiefs by saying that it would be done later when the task of again having the reserve boundaries agreed to.

As a joint commission, it operated between 1876 and 1878. Later it was changed to a single person commission operated by Gilbert Sproat between 1878 and 1880. From 1880 to 1898, the commission was operated by Peter O'Reilly. Between 1898 to 1910, when it ended, the commission was headed by A.W. Vowell.

Reserves boundaries were again pointed out for Okanagan, Arrow Lakes, Penticton, Douglas Lake, Similkameen, and Osoyoos by the Chiefs. In addition, three areas would be **allowed** common usage by settlers on lands which were in the original Douglas reserves. It did not sell, surrender or cede lands to the Crown. It simply allowed settlers to graze on reserve lands without the usual trespass. In fact it was a tool which recognized the ownership of the Okanagan by its creation.

The North Okanagan commonage reserve allotted Oct. 15, 1877, lay between the eastern shore of Okanagan Lake and Kalamalka and Wood Lakes, surveyed at 24,742 acres. This commonage was opened up for settlement by a Dominion Order-in-Council, January 5, 1889, without asking or telling the Okanagans as they had done to get commonage rights. No compensation was ever made.

The South Okanagan Commonage reserve was allotted on Nov. 24, 1877. It was recorded as being between Trout Creek on the south and Trepanier Creek to the north, and from the west shore of Okanagan Lake to a line two miles to the west of the old Hudson's Bay Brigade trail. This commonage was not surveyed but had around 30,000 acres inside very clear boundaries. The same privy council order used to open the North Okanagan Commonage was used to steal the southern commonage.

The Douglas Lake commonage reserve was allotted by Sproat on September 28, 1878, and lay to the north and east of Douglas Lake. It was surveyed at 18,553 acres. No order-in-council opening it up was ever issued.

In 1878, Gilbert Malcolm Sproat became the sole Indian Reserve Commissioner, but he resigned in 1880 because he disagreed with control placed on his allotments of reserves. The province **claimed** to have the right **to disapprove** any of the reserves allotted by Sproat. It was a right disputed by the Federal Government. It was not a right stated in the orders-in-council for the commission. The province had **no legal say** in the matter. The Federal Government clearly had **the only** legal duty and say in the matter of "Indian lands."

In Similkameen, the reserve allotted by Commissioner Sproat had stretched unbroken from two miles below the Ashnola River to the U.S. line on both sides of the river. Because of this allotment and other fair agreements for the size of reserves, the Province tried to stop the work of the Commission.

From 1880 to 1898, Peter O'Reilly was made head of the Indian reserve commission. In 1884 O'Reilly revisited the Similkameen and cut down Sproat's reserve and allotted a much smaller reserve. O'Reilly lied to the band and said that their long reserve had only been "temporary" and had been taken back by the province. That is called fraud. The reserve had been legally allotted. He also ruled that an additional 550 acres of reserve had been claimed by a white settler and could no longer be reserve. That was also illegal. As well, the Department of Lands used that opportunity to further cancel lands allotted to Lower Similkameen, lots 555 and 556, which included about half the present townsite of Cawston. None of this was legal process which required **consent**.

In Osoyoos, Sproat's allotment in 1877 included all the bottom land on the east bank of the Okanagan River. In the years before the reserve was officially surveyed, the province "**sold**" some of the most valuable and fertile land along the river. The lands were sold with the help of Judge W. Haynes, a local government official of the Lands Department. He had also helped in the Trutch reductions. It is certainly no accident that Haynes wound up owning much of that land and definitely in conflict of interest. Selling land unsurrendered and unceded remains a definite legal question.

An Arrow Lakes Reserve on the west shore of Lower Arrow Lake, about five miles below Burton, allotted by Commissioner Vowell, October 10, 1902, was surveyed in 1902 at 255 acres. In 1953, upon the death of Annie Joseph, the reserve was said to be cancelled. It was transferred in 1938 under Order-in-council 1036 (a provincial order) which said that reserve lands must "**revert**" to the province if the Indians on it became extinct.

A presumed ownership by the province exists in that order-in-council. In fact the original people of the Okanagan as a Nation are the only owners of all lands unceded and not treated since the larger question of underlying title has **never** been settled. The extinction clause was amended in 1969 at which time it was removed. The Arrow Lakes reserve still belongs to the Arrow Lakes Okanagan descendants who are now dispersed on every reserve of the Okanagan in Canada and the US.

The Reserve Commission officially ended in 1910. In 1910 Vowell wrote that the province had refused to sanction any further allotments of land to Indians and that the work of the Commission "... cannot...proceed" until a settlement between the two governments could be reached.

SCHEDULE OF RESERVES AS REPORTED IN THE 1902 DIA SUPPLEMENT TO THE ANNUAL REPORT (SEE APPENDIX)

As during the visits of the Commission and after, the Chiefs continued to push for the settlement of the larger question, mostly because of being denied the right to use their territories for hunting, fishing, food gathering, grazing, water and timber resources. By then many Okanagan were farming and logging as well as continuing to hunt, fish and gather traditional foods.

LIST OF OKANAGAN CHIEFS IN DIA ANNUAL REPORT 1900

Name	Rank	Appointed or Elected	From what Date	Term
OKANAGAN AGENCY				
Ashnola Band-John	Chief	Elected	1866	Life
Chuchuwayha Band- Moise	Chief	Elected	1867	Life
Hamilton Creek Band-Michel				Life
KeremeusBand Nkamaplix Band- Jouie Jim	Chief	Elected	April, 1898	3 years
Duck Lake Band- Enoch	Chief			Recognized as Chief for Many Years
Okanagan Lake Band-Charles	Chief	Elected		Life
Nkamip Band (Osoyoos)-Gregoire	Chief	Elected	1870	Life
Penticton Band-Francois	Chief	Elected	1864	Life
Shennoskuanki Band- Joseph	Chief			Life
Spahamin Band (Douglas Lake)- John Chilhusta (suc. father)	Chief	Elected	1885	Life

In 1906, there is a documented report of a delegation of four chiefs, headed by Okanagan Chief Chilheetza and accompanied by Atum and two others, to see Sir Wilfred Laurier. Oral reports document that Chief Chilheetza, Chief Atum, Chief Basil, and one other Chief of the Okanagan or Shuswap also went to England to petition King George III that same year. At the same time a similar delegation of Squamish Chiefs went to explain their grievances. Their petition is said to have contained four points in relation to title and rights. (Reverend O'Meara, report of the Friends of the Indians)

Chief Manual Louie, Chief George Baptiste (Che' nut) and Chief Narcisse Baptiste. Picture taken in Spences Bridge, BC.

National Museums of Canada.

In 1909, another delegation representing twenty tribes, from the coast and Southern Interior went to London with a similar petition. They also visited Ottawa. (The Indian Land Claims Struggle in British Columbia: a brief history, Beth Van Dyke, Doug Saunders, 1975).

In 1910, the Four Interior Tribes, the Okanagan, the Shuswap, the Thompson, and the Lillooet signed a declaration petitioning Sir Wilfred Laurier, Prime Minister of Canada. They declared the position on their rights and their problems with British Columbia.

. . . We expect much of you as the head of this great Canadian nation, and feel confident that you will see that we receive fair and honourable treatment. . . . we hope that with your help our wrongs may at last be righted. We speak to you the more freely because you are a member of the white race with whom we first became acquainted, and which we call in our tongue "real whites." . . . The "real whites" we found were good people. We could depend on their word, and we trusted and respected them. They did not interfere with us nor attempt to break up our tribal organizations, laws and customs. They did not try to force their conceptions of things on us to our harm. Nor did they stop us from catching fish, hunting, etc. They never tried to steal or appropriate our country, nor take our food and life from us. They acknowledged our ownership of the country, and treated our chiefs as men. . . . Because of this we have a warm heart to the French at the present day. . . . When they first came among us there were only Indians here. They found the people of each tribe supreme in their own territory, and having tribal boundaries known and recognized by all. . . . We wish just to pass over your lands in quest of gold." Soon they saw the country was good, and some of them made up their minds to settle in it. They commenced to take up pieces of land here and there. . . .At this time they did not deny the Indian tribes owned the whole country and everything in it. . . . We trusted the whites and waited patiently for their chiefs to declare their intentions toward us and our lands. . . . They told us to have no fear, and queen's laws would prevail in this country, and everything would be well for the Indians here. They said a very large reservation would be staked off for us (southern interior tribes) and the tribal lands outside of this reservation the government would buy from us for white settlement. They let us think this would be done soon, and meanwhile until this reserve was set apart, and our lands settled for, they assure us we would have perfect freedom of travelling and camping and the same liberties as from time immemorial to hunt, fish, graze and gather our food supplies wherever we desired; also that all trails, land, water, timber, etc., would be as free of access to us as formerly. Our chiefs were agreeable to these propositions, so we waited for treaties to be made, and everything settled. . . . They treat us as subjects without any agreement to that effect, and force their laws on us without our consent, and irrespective of whether they are good for us or not. . . . They have taken possession of all the Indian country and claim it as their own. . . . we never accepted these reservations as settlement for anything, nor did we sign any papers or make any treaties about same. . . . We have always felt the injustice done us, but we did not know how to obtain redress. . . . we can see we will go to the wall, and most of us be reduced to beggary or to continuous wage slavery. We have also learned lately that the British Columbia government claims absolute ownership of our reservations, which means that we are practically landless. . . . We condemn the whole policy of the B.C. Government towards the Indian tribes of this country as utterly unjust, shameful and blundering in every way. . . . So long as what we consider justice is withheld from us, so long will dissatisfaction and unrest exist among us, and we will continue to struggle to better ourselves. . . . We demand that our land question be settled, and ask that treaties be made between the government and each of our tribes, in the same manner as accomplished with the Indian tribes of the other provinces of Canada, and the neighbouring parts of the United States.

Sir Wilfred Laurier met with a delegation of British Columbia Chiefs at Prince Rupert and Kamloops in order to hear their grievances about rights and title. In a strong action never seen before or since, Sir Wilfred Laurier answered in 1910, by preparing a set of ten questions that the courts could hear on the matter. Three of these concerned title directly. The remainder dealt with size of reserves, reversionary interest and grievances with respect to reserves.

The legal questions were prepared by the Federal Department of Justice and **approved** by the Attorney-General of Canada. Legal officers of the province also helped in preparing and agreed to the questions. However the Provincial Government under Richard McBride **refused** to go to court on the question of aboriginal title. Refusal to go to court is contempt of justice.

Again the Laurier's Government took action to live up to its duty. It amended the Indian Act to allow the legal case to move forward. On May 17, 1911, the Laurier Government passed a Dominion Order-In-Council which **ordered** the Exchequer Court of Canada to begin legal proceedings on behalf of the Indians of B.C.

In September of 1911, Sir Wilfred Laurier's Liberal government was defeated by the Conservatives. Robert Borden became the Prime Minister of Canada. The federal attitude toward Richard McBride's Conservative provincial government changed rapidly.

"The order-in-council was never enforced and legal action was never taken against British Columbia. New talks to settle the disputes began in 1912 between the two **Conservative** governments. The response of Borden's government was to appoint yet another Royal Commissioner in 1912 in the person of J. A. McKenna to negotiate with the province to settle the matter **"once and for all."** The negotiations led directly to the McKenna-McBride Agreement. It was commissioned to **adjust** the reserves allotted by the previous commission.

From 1913 to 1916, the McKenna-McBride Commission travelled throughout B.C. hearing evidence from Chiefs, Band Spokesmen, Indian Agents, white business groups, and others. Under the terms of the agreement reductions were to be made only with the consent of the Indians concerned. The commission had the power to allot additional lands for reserve.

The position of the Okanagan Chiefs is clear from their statements taken from the Royal Commission on Indian Affairs October 8, 1913, meeting at Penticton Indian Reserve.

HIGH CHIEF JOHN CHILHEETSA' STATEMENT

Chief John Chilheetsa, of Douglas Lake, spoke through the medium of the interpreter. He said, "Great White Chief, I come here as representing all these people. I wish to speak to you. I wish to hear from you as to whether this country belongs to you and your Government or to the Indians. I came here specially to hear that question answered. If you claim it is your country then we are of opposite opinions and I am opposed to that view. The Indians say that it is their country and if you claim it they want to go to some big court house and have the matter settled.

Chief Edward Michel of Penticton said "I love my land. I would like to say that we would not like to have this land cut off. We have no land to spare on this reserve."

Francois Timoykin said, "the Indians used to get their living from their land, and from God Almighty on the land, just like their fathers...It is not because the whiteman has come that we make a living - we have been living before the whiteman came and now you ask us how we get along. We get along from the land - it is our father and mother - we get our living just like milk from the land, therefore, we have no land to sell - it would be just like selling our bodies. We cannot sell any land until the Man who made the land comes back."

MEETING WITH THE SPULMACHEEN OR ENDERBY BAND OR INDI-ANS ON THEIR RESERVE AT ENDERBY, B.C. OCTOBER 2ND, 1913.

Chief Edward Clemah, addressed the Commissioners as follows: ". . . The Queen a long time ago put posts in this Reserve and said, 'We are done. This is your land', and she said that no one was to break this. She also said that you Indians and whitemen were to work peaceably all the time, and that is the reason I am making you a Reserve."

Chief Nahumcheen addressed the commission as follows: ". . I love all my land here. I have no hard feelings because this land has been fixed already. My father and the Queen have fixed this land. The Indians have business to talk about the land that is outside the Reserves. We came to the conclusion at that time to go to Victoria to talk about the land outside the Reserves. . . . There was 104 Chiefs went down and visited McBride at that time. After we got in we said, 'We want to ask you about this land, we want to know whether this land belongs to us or whether it belongs to you. . . ' At that time he was not able to tell us . . . He also said that land you got in your own hands and this land outside the Reserves I can't fix myself. I am not the Head Chief for that. Ottawa has not got the power to fix it. We are all working for the King - anything we want to do we name the King . ."

Chief Ashnola John addressed, "I have business to talk about my land outside the Reserves. . . the land that is outside of the Reserves now; we always use that land before just like our father and mother - we go there to camp, and are glad to go to these places. We are not saying that we don't want the whitemen or that the whitemen should not have the land . . ."

MEETING WITH THE DISTIKEPTUM BAND OF INDIANS ON THEIR NO. 9 OKANAGAN INDIAN RESERVE

Chief Charles, "I don't want to sell my land and I don't want any land to be cut up. I have no land to spare, and I have no land short. I am not short of land - my land continues right down to the shores of the big water, right down to the salt water - All the mountains and all the land is all good - The Indians all own it . . ."

When the Commission issued its report in 1916, it recommended that cutoffs be made from 54 reserves in total to accommodate the settlers who wanted those lands. Before the report became law this was lowered to 35 reserves totalling about 36,000 acres, most of it in the Okanagan.

As though that were not enough, the lands cutoff from the reserves were not the only lands taken away by the Commission. All lands that were in the railway belt were ordered cutoff. All lands included in the interim reports as rights-of way, under section 8 of the McKenna McBride Agreement were also ordered cutoff. Most of the Interim reports contain a phrase saying that **due compensation** must be made for the lands so taken.

After the Commission had completed its work, there were protests that too much land had been given to the Indians. W.E. Ditchburn from the Federal Government and Col J.W. Clark from the province were appointed to **review** the report. They made further changes to boundaries and even in some cases to the decisions made by McKenna/McBride.

The Okanagan Chiefs **did not give consent** and dissatisfaction was shown by them over the following years. The formation of the Allied Tribes by Andrew Paul from Squamish led to continued protest and resistance over the next 30 years. The Okanagan Chiefs sent many delegations to Victoria and Ottawa during that period to seek recognition in their position of sovereign title and rights. In 1926 the Allied Tribes was able to get a hearing granted by the Privy Council on the B.C. land question.

In response, Parliament established a Joint Committee to hold hearings and to make recommendations which would bring a resolution to the situation. The outcome of the Joint Committee hearings of 1927 is well known. The Committee said that the Allied Tribes and the Indians of B.C. had not proven their claims. However, the Committee made recommendations on other claims for social and economic problems. They recommended an annual special vote of $100,000 to be made by Parliament to be expended for the improvement of Indian life in the province. This is known as the B.C. special.

The strongest decision of the Joint Committee was a resolution, later made law, that the raising of funds by Indian organizations to press for the settlement of the land question was a criminal offence. This marked the death of the Allied Tribes of B.C. as an organization representing the Indians of B.C.

In 1931 the Native Brotherhood of B.C. was established and a petition was submitted to the Minister of the Interior to represent the grievances. It fell on deaf ears.

In 1938, the Federal Government and the Province of B.C. reached a settlement and Order-in-Council 1036 was passed. The Order-in-Council was to "convey" title of Indian reserves in the province to the Federal Government, with the province keeping the right to "resume" title over rights-of-way and to 1/20 of "unused reserve lands" for that purpose.

This order-in-council is a serious breach of trust by the Federal Government because it presumes a prior legal title of the province without surrender of those lands even to the Crown. The Federal Government has a clear legal duty to **first** get the lands by Treaty for the Crown **before** the province has any say on the lands at all.

From 1931 up to 1969 the Okanagan Chiefs and people were active in the Native Brotherhood and the North American Indian Brotherhood, in the struggle with the governments of Canada and the Province.

In 1931 the Statute of Westminster gave the Dominion of Canada the power to make laws. Section 7(1) of the statute outlines the obligations which were vested in the Imperial Crown through the British North America Act and the areas of the statutes' applications. The Statute of Westminster does not give Canada or the provinces the right to breach the Imperial Crown's trust in its duties with those laws. The laws of Canada cannot supersede the Crown's legal duty in any matter.

During the war years reserve lands were taken without payment for army bases, airports, and later for grants to returning veterans. Much of these lands were taken under the War Measures Act and other instruments. These have not been legally clarified and researched.

SOME LIES COME OUT

In 1965, the Supreme Court of Canada rendered a decision on Regina VS White and Bob, a case on southern Vancouver Island in which two Indians were prosecuted for hunting deer. The defence was based on aboriginal rights. It avoided the question to land title but upheld the Colonial period treaties of Sir James Douglas for the right to hunt and fish. The decision is significant.

In June of 1969, the new Liberal government in Ottawa issued a White Paper on Indian Affairs. It was a proposed plan for the termination of Indian reserves. It clearly stated a policy not to recognize aboriginal land claims. Pierre Trudeau, Prime Minister, said in Vancouver, "We can't recognize aboriginal rights because no society can be built on historical 'might have beens.' "

B.C. Indians immediately formed a response movement. The result was the formation of the Union of B.C. Indian Chiefs, as an organization resisting the attempts of the government to go with this policy. The Union of B.C. Indian Chiefs continues to the present in its endeavour to respond politically to the government's schemes.

In February 1973, the Supreme Court of Canada ruled on the Nisgha case which was based on underlying title. A split decision of the Supreme Court Judges was handed down. The most important part of the finding was that the judges ruled that the Aboriginal people had original title recognized under English law. Three of the judges ruled that extinguishment of title could not be proven and further that extinguishment must be clearly written into statute (legislated acts) law. The court stayed tied on that issue.

Shortly after, an all party standing committee of Parliament on Indian Affairs passed a motion that approved the extinguishment of land claims in regions where treaties had not already extinguished aboriginal title. In August of 1973 Jean Chretien announced that the Federal Government intended to **settle** lands claims in all parts of Canada where no treaties had been made. The policy was to extinguish original title by paying for it.

In 1975 the province of B.C., the Federal Government and twenty-three bands who had lands illegally cut off by the McKenna McBride Commission jointly agreed to a negotiated process for settlement rather than to go to court.

In 1979, Justice Mahoney, in the Baker Lake case said there were four things which an Aboriginal group could show to prove Aboriginal title. They were:

(1) Them or their ancestors were members of an organized society.

(2) The organized society occupied the specific territory over which they assert Aboriginal title.

(3) The occupation was to the exclusion of other organized societies

(4) The occupation was an established fact at the time sovereignty was asserted by England.

The Baker Lake and the Nisgha cases made clear that corporations trespassing on unsurrendered lands could be challenged legally. It meant that the licences which the government was issuing for mining, forestry, and other damage could be stopped with a court injunction showing that an Aboriginal Nation had some proof of the four points.

As a result, many companies that would be affected (many of them Crown Corporations) stated their concerns to the Federal and Provincial governments. Of course this meant loss of votes if nothing was done to allow the companies freedom to continue to exploit Aboriginal lands.

In short order, the Government of Canada announced its intent to bring home the Constitution from British control. With a new constitution the Government could find ways along its own voters' interests to end treaty and Aboriginal rights and continue the damage to the environment.

In 1982 Britain passed the Canada Act which would allow Canada to make its own constitution. Making a Canadian Constitution would remove from Britain the duty for the rights of the Canadian people of Canada. It would allow for new relationships with each of the different groups in Canada that has legal right for protection of rights which were historically guaranteed to them.

The Canada Act is a binding agreement by Canada to Britain that it will not destroy the rights of the peoples of Canada which Britain had legal duty for in the treaties and charters and acts that it had made in the past. It does not automatically give Canada the right to change any of those past agreements and commitments. In fact it enforces and protects them. Canada can only change them by the **consent** of groups involved.

Groups which could have claimed a historical right to take equal part in making decisions over how Canada will operate to protect their separate rights are:

- The provinces from provincial acts and terms of Confederation

- The territories from territorial acts after Confederation

- Quebec from the Quebec Act before Confederation

- Riel's people from the Manitoba Act

- Treaties from before Confederation and the Canada Act

- Treaties from after Confederation and the Canada Act

- Aboriginal Nations without treaties from 1763 Royal Proclamation and "Existing Rights" Canada Act.

Neither CANADA or the provinces automatically have the right to disallow any of those groups to speak for **themselves**, whether they choose to come into the constitution or not. Recognition does not automatically mean to come into the constitution. It can mean a recognition of the relationship to Britain, or the right to **stay** separate from Canada with an international agreement of coexistence. Very small countries in Europe exist as separate entities this way.

CURRENT LIES

In the current years since 1982, the Governments of Canada and the provinces have ignored the history of their duty originating in the way the country was founded. Relying on past lies and deceits to further the injustice and continue the war of conquest of the Aboriginal Nations, the government has taken a position of refusing to recognize the sovereignty of the Aboriginal Nations, both those with and those without treaties, in the constitutional talks. The tools of war the government uses are to do studies, reviews, Royal Commissions, and Parliament Standing Committees, in the pretence of helping define "Existing Aboriginal and Treaty Rights." It uses these tools to find out how much the Aboriginal Nations know and what they want, so the "offers" can be worded close to what the Aboriginal Nations want. It is a way to find out which groups and individuals are more "willing" to see things their way and why.

In 1982, after attempts by Canada to leave out the Crown's duty to Aboriginal Peoples from the Canada Constitution Act, Aboriginal Nations from Alberta, Nova Scotia, and New Brunswick asked the English Court of Appeal to declare that the responsibility for Indians be left with the British Crown.

Although the request was denied, the judgement handed down by the British High court of Lord Denning described the Royal Proclamation of 1763 as "equivalent to an entrenched provision in the constitution of the colonies of North America." He held that it is binding on the crown "so long as the sun rises and the river flows."

"Its force as a statute, said Lord Denning, is the same as to the statutes of the Magna Carta, which has always been considered to be the law throughout the Empire." Lord Denning said that the **obligations** (legal duty) of the Crown under the Royal Proclamation of 1763 and under the pre-Confederation treaties signed with Aboriginal people, were undertaken with the passing of the BNA Act and were affirmed in their meaning.

He proposed that the Canadian constitution "does all that can be done to protect the **rights and freedoms** of the Aboriginal Peoples of Canada." He also said, "but if there should in future be **any** reason for distrust, then the discussion in this case will strengthen their hand so as to enable them to withstand **any** onslaught.... they will be able to say that their rights and freedoms **have been guaranteed to them by the Crown,** originally by the Crown in respect of the United Kingdom, now by the Crown in respect of Canada, but in **any** case, by the Crown. **No Parliament** should do **anything** to lessen the **worth** of these guarantees. They should be honoured by the Crown in respect of Canada 'so long as the sun rises and the river flows' that **promise must never be broken.**"

The Penner Report (Report of the Special Committee on Self Government) which followed shortly after, was completed in 1983. The main idea taken out of the Penner report was for the government to coin the words "self-government" as a tool to mean self-administration. In the report, Bands stated they wanted "Indian Government," the right to exercise their inherited sovereign powers be recognized by the constitution. The areas they mentioned included land and water resources.

The Neilson Task Force recommended in October of 1985 a formula that would enable the Federal Government to begin to terminate its duty toward Aboriginal Nations. This was termed the Buffalo Jump paper. Its recommendations centred around manipulating tight budget control to get bands in line. It recommended severe cutbacks in DIA funding and increased fund transfers from federal to provincial pockets as a way to end DIA. This would help put in place the tools for the Provinces to eventually take full control over "Indian" affairs. Provinces have since created "Indian Affairs" branches to accommodate the federal transfers of money and programs.

The Buffalo Jump paper also outlined the government plan to redefine the term "Indian Self-Government" as municipal-style self-administration under existing Provincial jurisdiction. It outlined how the scheme could be sold and negotiated into the constitution through a step-by-step consent method using the budget cuts as a squeeze tactic. It outlined how alternate (block) funding would lead some (fit) bands to an agreement on self-government which could be passed without constitutional reform. These bands could trade over their sovereign powers before any definition of section 35 of the Canada Act.

In the Coolican Report of 1985 (Report to Review the Comprehensive Claims Policy), the main idea to come out was to accept more claims settlements to be approved per year and to widen the eligibility of claims and to deal with them quicker.

In the Oberle report of 1985, the main idea to come out was that a framework was needed to make rules for interpreting treaties. The terms used were, to restore "inherent self-government powers and titles and nationhood" in the intergovernmental relations with the Crown.

RECENT LEGAL CASES

A general tone of judgements in favour of Aboriginal Rights was set in the landmark Guerin Case of 1984. The Supreme Court of Canada held that the Federal Government has a fiduciary and trust-like obligation to First Nations when Indian lands are surrendered for lease or sale, and that, the fiduciary relationship between the Crown and Indians has its roots in the concept of Aboriginal, Native or Indian title.

Further enforcing this trend in Canadian Law, major decisions were won in 1990 opposing federal and provincial agencies and/or governments in court. The judgements in The Flett Case (in Manitoba) and The Sioui Case (in Quebec) both confirmed that Treaty rights override legislation and regulations.

But by far the most significant decision came on May 31, 1990, when the Supreme Court of Canada handed down the judgement in The Sparrow Case. It established several important aspects of Aboriginal Rights in Law. Among other things, Sparrow recognized that: extinguishment of Aboriginal title can only be achieved through legislation where the **intention to do so is clearly stated**; and, that the **onus is on**

the Crown to prove title has been extinguished; and, that the honour of the Crown is to be upheld in dealings with First Nations. According to the Rule of Law, these principles should have been reflected in policy and legislation without delay.

The Gitskan/Wet'suwet'en Case of Regina v. Delgamuuk, handed down in the Supreme Court of British Columbia on March 8, 1991, was completely opposite to the trend being set in Canadian Law. Justice Allen McEachern's judgement went against several previous rulings which recognized Aboriginal Title and Rights. The decision ignored most of the evidence presented in the case. It ruled that jurisdiction and rights had been extinguished prior to 1871. He ruled that the thirteen colonial proclamations and ordinances, which generally provided for the settlement of the new colony implied a "clear and plain" intention to extinguish all aboriginal interests. It appears to have been more a political/ economic decision rather a law decision, making a farce of the justice system.

On June 25, 1993, the British Columbia Court of Appeal released its decisions on the Delgamuuk case and seven other appeals in cases of related issues concerning the legal rights of British Columbia's Aboriginal Nations.

Three of the five Judges of the Court of Appeal agreed in rejecting the Gitskan claim to ownership and sovereignty. Two judges did not agree.

The Court of Appeal ruled that aboriginal rights are really only rights to occupy village sites and only shared rights in hunting, fishing and gathering foods in other parts of their territory. It ruled that these rights must be proven to be something central to the culture and it must have existed both in 1846 and in 1982.

The Court of Appeal did not agree that the colonial ordinances and proclamations satisfied the "clear and plain" test of the Sparrow case. The Appeal court also ruled that the Province of B.C. **does not** have constitutional power to extinguish aboriginal rights and that those rights are federal common law rights and therefore immune from derogation (cut down) by provincial law. It said that provincial laws can regulate aboriginal rights through section 88 of the Indian Act which makes provincial laws of general application apply, but also says that provincial laws may be rendered unconstitutional if they don't stay in line with the Constitution Act of 1982.

It acknowledged that the Province has full power to make valid grants of fee simple and lesser interests in lands and resources and that the grants made before 1982 cannot now be questioned. It said that a pre-1982 crown grant does not extinguish aboriginal rights but it might violate those rights and that an affected aboriginal Nation might recover damages or that the grant might be adjusted so it doesn't violate the aboriginal interest. It said that such crown grants made after 1982 might be made invalid by section 35 of the Constitution Act of 1982.

THE THREE PRONGED FORK IN THE TONGUE

- Consent by Constitutional Accord
- Consent by Legislation
- Consent by Claims Settlements

The question which all this brings us to is how legislative change, comprehensive land claims, and a constitutional definition of rights will affect the Sovereignty of Aboriginal Nations. Some bands say that Indian Act changes would be a good short term fix while we wait for a constitutional definition of rights. Some have said that Indian Act changes should not take place because it undermines the First Nations Assembly (an assembly of Indian band councils) agenda of a Constitutional definition of rights. In B.C., some bands say Indian Act changes should not take place until compensation settlement treaties are made. The Okanagan Elders say that all three actions are serious threats to the rights of our future generations and our sovereignty.

THE CONSTITUTIONAL TALKS

The sole intent in recent years has been to extinguish the duty the Canadian Government inherited from Britain. The duty is clearly spelled out in the Canada Act passed by Britain and in Lord Dennings statement. It says that **"existing aboriginal and treaty rights of the Aboriginal Peoples are hereby recognized and affirmed."**

The struggle in the past and in the present has been for the Aboriginal Nations to exercise the affirmed recognition of their rights in a way which protects their lands, their rights, and their peoples. Canada's underhanded interference and lack of political will stands as the biggest obstacle to that.

In the years since 1982 there have been different ways the government has tried to destroy "existing aboriginal and treaty rights." It is important to stay with the use of the words treaty and aboriginal, because they are the words which Britain used to make Canada legally responsible for the Crown's own original legal duty.

The main tool which the government used is by acting as though it did not have the legal duty to "affirm and recognize treaty and aboriginal rights." It insists that the aboriginal people are already somehow part of the Canadian Government and that they do not have a choice in the matter. Without a legal challenge, it has said that Aboriginal sovereignty is not an item to be discussed in the constitutional talks.

The government said it would not allow aboriginal people a voice at the First Ministers' meetings to decide what would go into the constitution to "affirm and recognize" rights which only the provinces and Canada would define. They said that the Provinces and the Federal Governments alone had the power to decide that. Clearly this gives power to the provinces, whose legal powers **never** have included "Indians or Indian lands" either under the BNA Act or the Canada Act.

The Provinces **do not** have powers over, or the same as, the Federal powers inherited from Britain, in those matters. The underlying federal authority to affirm and recognize "existing treaty and aboriginal rights" is the **only** authority inherited by Canada's Federal power from Britain, unless the Aboriginal Nations can be convinced to consent otherwise.

The "existing treaty and aboriginal rights" flowing from the Royal Proclamation are Aboriginal Nation Rights insuring a peaceful relationship next to territories surrendered to the Crown. The "Treaty Rights" are a legal responsibility of Canada to continue to pay the agreed benefits in compensation for lands surrendered to the Crown. The "Aboriginal Rights" are a legal responsibility of Canada to carry out the Federal Government's inherited duty to the Crown from the Royal Proclamation, where Treaties do not exist.

Canada uses the Provinces in a bully and scare tactic to make Aboriginal Nations feel that they **must** be allowed to **negotiate** their rights from a "Citizen of Canada" position as a "level" of government within Canada as though it did not have its own sovereign rights.

Aboriginal Nations have and hold secure their rights, whether they have entered into Treaty or not. The rights are recognized and affirmed by the Crown in the treaties (whether written, oral or recorded in Wampum) with Britain and in the legal mandate of the Royal Proclamation. The rights are not "given" by these tools to Aboriginal Nations; these tools simply obligate the Crown and Canada in its legal actions with regard to Aboriginal Nations.

The government uses the tactic that "First Nations" must be one big unit in their request for the "entrenchment" of their rights into the constitution. The Government said that "First Nations" must all agree on a definition of rights to be entrenched. As though groups somehow must conform to one definition for Canada's convenience. As though Aboriginal rights had to be defined in the constitution in order to "exist."

It proposed entrenchment of a "framework" of self-government by which "First Nations" could negotiate the "specifics" of their rights after the constitution was passed. The use of the words "First Nations" to mean individual village band councils is clearly a way to pretend that the Royal Proclamation is being respected when it really is a tool to get the consent of Aboriginal Nations to come under the constitution. To be part of Canada by consent.

The government says it wants the Aboriginal groups to have their "rights" entrenched in the constitution, but only in the frame that government decides. It says that only after the aboriginal people have "consented" to entrench their rights, will they make a final agreement that spells out what exactly those rights might be with each "First Nation." In other words, once the Aboriginal groups hand over their rights, then the government will tell them what rights they can have in the "new relationship."

In 1982, the National Indian Brotherhood underwent a change in structure. They reorganized themselves as **an Assembly of Band Councils as defined under the Indian Act** and called themselves the Assembly of "First Nations." Clearly village authorities such as Band Councils, trying to get "recognition and affirmation" as a Nation is as ridiculous as town councils with their Mayors attempting to act as "Nations." A village council does **not** meet the legal international criteria for nationhood.

Village councils cannot do much more than worry about their jobless poverty situations which threaten political positions every two years. These conditions can be used in the war against Aboriginal Nations.

The Government insisting that Village Band Councils are the only authorities that have any "recognized" voice in the talks is a tactic to dissolve Aboriginal Nations into many weak splinter groups. This is the first indication that Aboriginal Treaty Nation Groups and Non-Treaty Aboriginal Nation Groups are being attacked from an inside track through individual bands and individual persons. The powers of actual Nation Groups are being attacked and taken apart because this level is where the Nation Powers are held.

It is the first indication that **Bands** are being paid cheap lip service by the Government, as the "Nation" and being "given" authority and recognition as decision makers, as though they were Nations. In this way they cannot legally meet the criteria of being Aboriginal Nations as identified in the Royal Proclamation and in the Baker Lake Case and by the United Nations definition of what constitutes a Nation. This works only to the advantage of the Government scheme to limit or terminate the "existing treaty and aboriginal rights".

The economic despair of **bands** and the results in all the terrible social ills are ways to get Aboriginal people to consent to trading their National Trust (sovereignty and title) in for the power to sign cheques and a few more dollars yearly.

MEECH LAKE ACCORD

The would-be changes to the constitution drafted in 1987, held no favours for Aboriginal Peoples. The Accord would have ended Aboriginal Nation rights by giving powers to provinces over "Native Affairs," within the framework of a municipal level of "Indian Self-Government." It also gave provinces (especially Quebec) the right to block further changes, including how First Nation rights and self-determination would be defined. Meech would have made any defining amendments next to impossible, creating a total block to aboriginal constitutional matters.

For this and other reasons, the stalling tactics over the passage of the Accord played out in the Manitoba Legislature were important. A low-profile MLA, Elijah Harper, along with the Assembly of Manitoba Chiefs, found themselves sitting around a table while the Prime Minister and his hard-hitters tried to offer a Royal Commission (groan) on Native Affairs to tempt a change of mind about blocking the passage of the Accord.

However, the offer was seen as being promised purely out of politics and not out of sincere intent. Later, it was clear that the right decision was made when appeals to hold the Royal Commission after the Accord's downfall, fell on deaf Federal ears. Aboriginal Nations did not exactly jump for joy at the Prime Minister's announcement of a Royal Commission on Aboriginal People in April of 1991.

The 1990 summer of the failure of Meech Lake gave Quebec many reasons to be resentful to the Federal Government and to Native Nations. It will be remembered in the memories of Native peoples as the summer that Elijah Harper found himself in a key position to serve the people to defeat the Accord. It is also remembered as the summer of backlash when the police force of Quebec, attacked the Mohawk people on the direction of the Mayor of Oka who wished to build a golf course on traditional Mohawk land. It is remembered as a summer of Canadian shame, when the Canadian Armed forces were brought in to assist the move to push provincial powers onto sovereign Mohawk territory.

CHARLOTTETOWN ACCORD

The Federal Government's 1992 Constitutional proposal made public in September, 1991, was coined as, "Shaping Canada's Future Together". It offered little more than the Meech Lake proposal with regard to what Aboriginal Nations have guaranteed to them in the Canada Act. The Federal Government's previous indication that it might consider having "First Nation" Representatives sit at the table as equals for negotiations, did not happen.

The Accord offered some seats in the Senate to be set aside for Aboriginal Senators who have no decision making power or ability to affect change in policy. The Accord offered again an "inherent right to Indian self-government" in a framework which could be negotiated band by band over the next five years, if they agreed not to go to court over that period, over any rights. It offered a recognition of the Metis as a "First Nation".

Canada once again refused to consider simply recognizing powers of Aboriginal Nations and their sovereign rights and title. The proposal spoke of the justifiable right to Self-Government, which is interpreted to mean that First Nation Self-Governments cannot override other existing jurisdictions. The Charlottetown Accord was not accepted.

LEGISLATED CONSENT

Three things that happened in recent years are important to look at in the Government of Canada's inherited duty towards the Aboriginal Peoples.

First, in the Guerin Case of 1984, the judgement of the Supreme Court of Canada said that DIA has a "fiduciary (trusteeship) and trust-like" duty when Indian lands are surrendered for lease or sale, and that, the fiduciary relationship between the Crown and Indians has its roots in the concept of Aboriginal, Native or Indian title . . ." The settlement awarded by the courts to the band was large.

Second, in the Auditor Generals Report in 1986, it was recommended, among other things, that DIA should review its legal duties. In particular, it should review how to carry out its duties with Indian land management, estate management and Band funds administered through the Indian Act. The dollar **cost** of carrying out these legal duties is a big thing with the government (it ends up costing votes).

Third, in the 1988 Report of the Commission of Inquiry Concerning Matters Associated with the Westbank Indian Band, it was recommended that the Indian Act be changed and become more in line with what they were proposing to do with their Indian self-government scheme.

Under pressure by these and other related things, TREASURY BOARD began a major review of LANDS, RESERVES AND TRUSTS in 1987. The main purpose was to come up with changes in legislation to replace those parts of the Indian Act which were legally in the way of the government's scheme. In 1988, DIA took over the Review itself. This was known as the **LRT** Review.

The government's decision to do the LRT Review was to find ways to protect itself from being found, again, to not legally be doing its Fiduciary (trust) duty as in the Guerin Case. The easiest way for the Government was to try to make changes which would prevent more legal judgements forcing fair settlements for the Indian lands it sells. The LRT review was the tool used to do more than "review" the trust duty it has.

The best way is obvious. It would be in limiting or cutting out altogether the legal trust duty towards aboriginal groups and to transfer the responsibility for this duty by the aboriginal groups' own consent. At the same time as achieving this, the government could use the LRT Review to look like they were listening to concerns about the Indian Act and seem to be taking the direction of Indian bands.

Offering things that we most need are ways to force us to consent to "negotiate" our rights away. The LRT Review is a longer termed plan than it appears on the surface. It is a process involving the best of these war tools. It is a three-staged process to terminating the Government of Canada's Trust relationship.

The DIAND LRT Review, outlined three phases it would use to change legislation (the Indian Act).

Phase 1: study the weakness of the Lands, Trusts and Reserves sections of the Indian Act and find problems and issues around them which Indian bands want most to change

Phase 2: study Phase 1 issues and propose options for changes

Phase 3: negotiate and implement the changes

The Phase 1 Report was released in 1988 and covered the following 7 areas which were found by the Department to contain problems in the Indian Act:

1) Land Management

2) Land Registry

3) Moneys

4) Estates

5) Band By-Laws

6) Elections

7) Membership

DIA said that upon finishing Phase 2, Indian Bands would be "consulted" before changes to the Indian Act would be put in place in Phase 3.

The first two stages of the review were carried through with very little input. DIA designed the workplan for the LRT Review and hired white consultants to identify the areas of study to be included in the Phase I Report to be the main points throughout the Review. Phase 2, which studied problems and issues and looked at options for changes, was done with token input from a few hand-picked bands and people chosen by DIA.

Through its LRT Review workplan, DIA proposed that the majority of Bands would be consulted only when all the areas of study had been identified and reviewed, and once all options for change have already been set out.

The way in which the LRT Review was carried out shows how the Federal Government interprets its trust duty to our Nations. It shows that the Government believes that it can take control. It thinks it can make changes in the trust duty in a sly way without the consent of Aboriginal Nations.

Even though the words "Indian self-government", are used in its scheme, the Federal Government holds onto its position that they control Aboriginal Nations. The old tool or **legislation** by which they controlled, is called the Indian Act. Changing the Indian Act is part of the three-staged scheme of the LRT review to terminate Canada's duty.

Although the Indian Act is a tool by which the government controls, it also sets out their **legal** duty to the Queen's Treaties and Agreements. This legal duty is the Lands, Reserves and Trusts. It is these "trust responsibilities" in the Indian Act which protects the treaties and lands and aboriginal rights in Canada's legal duty. It is the part that the Government **does not** control. It is controlled by the agreements of the Crown to our ancestors. It is the historical relationship of our Nations to the Crown. Canada as the Crown is governed by the past legal agreements made by the British Crown, even in the Indian Act.

The Indian Act, **legally,** should simply have been a legislated recognition of treaties and obligations which come out of them and a recognition of Aboriginal rights in territories where no treaties had been made and a way to fulfil the Royal Proclamations legal command.

Internal matters such as our membership, our laws, our social programs, our governance and elections and finances are not Canada's business or legal "trust duty" to the Crown. These are tools of control and genocide. These "non-trust responsibilities" are simply money policies passed by parliament and can be changed **at will** by legislation. They also can be interpreted financially **at will** by the Minister of Indian Affairs for any purposes they decide. There exist good recent examples of use of financial control to block attempts by bands to question this illegal practice by "cutting" or "capping" funds.

We all know our poverty and our needs for education, housing and health and jobs are used to create a "program" dependency on DIA. Those severe needs for our survival are used in a wicked sly way to control us toward giving up our sovereign treaty and aboriginal rights which Canada is **obligated** to recognize and which is **not** a matter of political policy or will.

There continues to be high numbers of young suicides and deaths from violence and drugs and alcohol. There are high numbers of infant deaths and adult deaths from diabetes and heart disease because of poor diet. The situation is desperate because of poverty and lack of education and cultural racism. This despair and poverty is what is used to control us toward handing over our sovereignty and rights. This kind of **control** over the very lives of people is called **Genocide**. The Convention against Genocide is one of the Universal Laws of the United Nations which Canada and Britain is bound by C and E of Article 2 of the convention have been violated as follows:

C) Deliberately inflicting on the group conditions of life calculated to bring about its physical destruction in whole or in part;

E) Forcibly transferring children of the group to another group.

Article 4)
Persons committing genocide or any of the other acts enumerated in Article 3 shall be punished, whether they are constitutionally responsible rulers, public officials or private individuals.

WHAT WE DON'T ACCOMPLISH TODAY
OUR CHILDREN WILL INHERIT.

There are cases which have not had wide publicity of high up Indian Affairs officials being charged for creating ways in which money was shuffled through a band to their companies through consultants and real estate business. There are cases in which band members have asked for special inquiries into the conflicts of interest of the DIA and band elected officials. There are instances right across Canada of economic development project monies being channelled toward creating a few "millionaire" Chiefs and individuals who are then used by DIA to push their membership into going along with the government's plan. The plan to dissolve its "trust duties" over which it has no control, into legislations over which it has solid control.

The "existing treaty and aboriginal right" is that " legal trust duty" which they must have **consent** from the aboriginal nations to change or terminate. It is that which they are trying to capture by "agreeing" to change the parts of the Indian Act which control our lives. It is that **legal duty** which must be recognized and protected **"Affirming Existing Treaty and Aboriginal Rights"** and not the Indian Act itself that must be protected.

The bait being offered is less control administratively. In an act which already presents serious legal questions of discrimination and human rights violation. Whatever happens to the Indian Act, the **legal duty** must not be changed. Previously mentioned Supreme Court decisions support that it **cannot** be changed without clear informed consent.

A "new" relationship with Canada is **not** necessary to "Affirm Existing Treaty and Aboriginal Rights". The "self-government" inclusion in the constitution is **not** necessary for this. The Lands, Trusts and Reserves review ending up in legislated changes to the Indian Act is **not** necessary to do this. The "extinguishment" of "Land Claims" is **not** necessary to do this.

These actions are a serious threat to recognizing and protecting these rights. These are hidden ways to get aboriginal consent to dissolve these rights in exchange for a little more self-administration and a little more money, both of which can be legislated away later.

Bands and individuals who support Indian Act legislative changes such as the **Optional Chartered Land Legislative Proposal for Specific Nations**, say such changes would lead to immediate increases in bands being able take lands out of the trust relationship and be able to develop and borrow on or lease or sell lands for monies. They say that the legislation to do this would allow them control over their lands. In fact, it will legally allow government laws to control those lands for the first time.

"**Recognition** of existing aboriginal and treaty rights" is the Crown's imposed mandate in the Canada Act. Unless Canada shifts its policy to recognize legally and politically, the sovereignty affirmed in existing treaties, and the sovereign rights of non-treaty aboriginal groups, there is not a fulfilment of that legal duty.

The only way for the government not to recognize it would be to get Aboriginal groups to **consent** to some other "relationship". That is exactly what it is trying to buy through deceit and power.

Only with the Guidance of our Elders
&
the Support of our People
can we Realize our Sovereignty.

The Okanagan Elders and people who stand for sovereignty along with other Aboriginal Nation groups say legislated changes being pushed through by Band elected officials selected and **paid** by the Federal Cabinet as special working groups are stopping any serious talks on forcing Canada to live up to its legal duty in the Canada Act.

In 1991 the Federal Government formed a Chiefs Governance Working Group comprised of hand-picked Band Council Chiefs and others who had demonstrated a desire to move on the federal scheme. The Working Group's stated objective is to change the relationship between Band Councils and the Crown. The main thrust seems to be finishing the work started in the LRT Review. This is being done by them negotiating with the Federal Government behind closed doors to approve amendments to the Indian Act and/or drafting new federal legislations to replace the Indian Act or parts of it.

LAND CLAIMS SETTLEMENTS

The British Columbia Government in the meantime was trying to buy away, piece by piece, the sovereign rights of Nations in their territories. Fisheries, forestry, and water rights are being taken as separate large pieces to be negotiated with committees of representatives rather than aboriginal nations.

The British Columbia Land Claims Task Force was formed in 1991 to resolve (again) the land question in BC. Before that the BC Social Credit government's position had always been not to discuss the issue of land claims. The Task Force was a Provincial Government quick solution to solve the reluctance of foreign investors in BC because of Aboriginal Nation militancy. There was also public pressure to deal with Aboriginal Nations and the pressure of court cases in favour of Aboriginal Nations.

Representatives from the Province, the Federal Government and Band Councils were appointed to the Task Force and mandated to make recommendations and submit a report. The Report was handed down in July, 1991. It contained no recognition of Aboriginal Title or change of the policy of extinguishment. It is worth noting that the Task Force's final work and the drafting of the report coincided almost perfectly with the early aftermath of the McEachern Decision where Aboriginal Nations rights in BC were severely attacked.

In 1992, the B.C. Treaty commission was put in place to carry out the work of negotiating treaties in B.C. within a frame of a three-party negotiated process. These are the Federal Government, the BC Government and the BC First Nations Summit. The framework protocol requires companion Acts by the Federal Government and the B.C. Government and resolutions by Band Councils representing themselves as "First Nations" in the Summit. Even though bands are not nations and British Columbia as a second level of government is not a nation, Band Councils are flocking to the "Treaty" negotiations.

A Royal Federal Indian Claims Commission is doing a similar exercise with the intent of amending the Federal Government's Land Claims Policy. This initiative came about as a result of Canada being forced to make desperate promises designed to change the relationship between Canada and Aboriginal Nations in the wake of the Mohawk Standoff. Again, this initiative is intended largely to make it look like Canada is listening to Aboriginal Nations. So far the government still refuses to remove the extinguishment of Aboriginal Title clause from the policy.

The Royal Commission on Aboriginal Peoples, announced by PM Mulroney in April of 1991, began touring across the country in 1992. The Commission was given the vague job to study (again) the broad issues concerning Aboriginal Peoples in Canada. Its stated goal is to bring about full participation in all aspects of Canadian life.

The Royal Commission released it's Partners in Confederation Report on Self-Government on August 18, 1993. It is in line with the Federal Government's policy on extinguishment of Aboriginal Rights.

Based on the past experience of the Penner Report of the Special Committee on Indian Self-Government (1983) and the Coolican Report (Report of the Task Force To Review Comprehensive Claims Policy -1986), the recommendations will be ignored and the report will be used to develop a new scheme for the next round of constitution talks.

In late 1992 the Mohawks who stood trial protecting their sovereignty and their land in 1990 against the Quebec provincial police and the Canadian army were acquitted. The Okanagan Nation supported their sovereignty stand with a peace run to Oka and a road block.

There are currently a number of proposed legislative initiatives in various stages of development and negotiation. These include;

- A proposed First Nation's Land Management Act

- A proposed First Nation's Governance Recognition Act

- A proposed First Nation's Forest, Lands and Resources Act

- A proposed First Nation's Government Finance Act

- A proposed First Nation's Government Taxation Act.

These initiatives are being proposed through the chief's governance working group under funding arrangment begun on 8th of April 1991. The chiefs governance working group's task as stated in the funding agreement is for the sole and express purpose of supporting and facilitating the development of the alternatives to the **Indian Act** in the area of governance.

In 1993 the relations between Canada and Quebec becomes even more strained as the failed constitutional talks begins to force Quebec to choose separation. The impending question will be Canada's Crown obligations to the Aboriginal Nations in Quebec.

As 1993 and the year of the Indigenous People comes to a close, the United Nations is developing a policy on the recognition of the political, cultural and economic rights of Indigenous Peoples. Canada, at the same time, is shamefully hurrying to deceitfully end its duty to Aboriginal Nations in their right to exist as Nations.

MOHAWK CRISIS 1990

APPENDIX

U.N. DRAFT DECLARATION

ON THE RIGHTS OF INDIGENOUS PEOPLES

The following is the draft of the declaration on the Rights of Indigenous Peoples as submitted by the Chairperson of the United Nations Working Group on Indigenous Populations, Ms. Erica-Irene Daes. This draft was the working paper for the discussions that took place during the summer of 1992 in Geneva, Switzerland.

During the discussions many nation-states and Indigenous Peoples offered suggestions on how to improve the declaration. Some nation-states, of course, tried to weaken the draft and Indigenous People and their supporters tried to strengthen it.

The Working Groups will consider all the suggestions and submit a revised draft for next year. It is expected that the United Nations will try to begin the process of ratifying the Declaration during 1993, The Year of Indigenous People.

Readers can evaluate for themselves the impact of such a declaration.

U.N. Draft Declaration on the Rights of Indigenous Peoples;

Affirming that all Indigenous peoples are free and equal in dignity and rights to all peoples in accordance with international standards, while recognizing the right of all individuals and peoples to be different, to consider themselves different, and to be respected as such.

Considering that all peoples contribute to the diversity and richness of civilizations and cultures, which constitute the common heritage of humankind.

Convinced that all doctrines, policies and practices of racial, religious, ethnic or cultural superiority are scientifically false, legally invalid, morally condemnable and socially unjust.

Concerned that Indigenous peoples have often been deprived of their human rights and fundamental freedoms, resulting in the dispossession of their lands, territories and resources, as well as in their poverty and marginalization.

Considering that treaties, agreements and other constructive arrangements between States and Indigenous peoples continue to be matters of international concern and responsibility.

Welcoming the fact that Indigenous peoples are organizing themselves in order to bring an end to all forms of discrimination and oppression wherever they occur.

Recognizing the urgent need to respect and promote the rights and characteristics of Indigenous peoples, especially their rights to their lands, territories and resources which stem from their history, philosophy, cultures and spiritual and other traditions, as well as from their political, economic and social structure.

Reaffirming that Indigenous peoples, in the exercise of their rights, should be free from adverse distinction of discrimination of any kind.

Endorsing efforts to revitalize and strengthen the societies, cultures and traditions of Indigenous peoples, through their control over development affecting them or their lands, territories and resources as well as to promote their future development in accordance with their aspirations and needs.

Recognizing that the lands and territories of Indigenous peoples should not be used for military purposes without their consent and affirming the importance of the demilitarization of their lands and territories which will contribute to peace, understanding, economic development and friendly relations among all peoples of the world.

Emphasizing the importance of giving special attention to the rights and needs of Indigenous women, youth and children, in particular to their right to equality of education opportunities and access to all levels and forms of education.

Recognizing in particular that it is usually in the best interest of Indigenous children for their family and community to retain shared responsibility for their upbringing and education.

Believing that Indigenous peoples have the right freely to determine their relationships with the States in which they live, in a spirit of coexistence with other citizens.

Noting that the International Covenants on Human Rights affirm the fundamental importance of the right of self-determination of all peoples, by virtue of which they freely determine their political status and freely pursue their economic, social and cultural development.

Bearing in mind that nothing in this Declaration may be used as an excuse for denying to any people its right of self-determination.

Encouraging States to comply with and effectively implement all international instruments as they apply to Indigenous peoples, in consultation with the peoples concerned.

Solemnly proclaims the following Declaration on the Rights of Indigenous Peoples.

1. Indigenous peoples have the right to self-determination, in accordance with international law by virtue of which they may freely determine their political status and institutions and freely pursue their economic, social and cultural development. An integral part of this is the right to autonomy and self-government.

2. Indigenous peoples have the right to the full and effective enjoyment of all of the human rights and fundamental freedoms which are recognized in the Charter of the United Nations and in international human rights law.

3. Indigenous peoples have the right to be free and equal to all other human beings and peoples in dignity and rights, and to be free from adverse distinction or discrimination of any kind based on their indigenous identity.

4. Nothing in this Declaration may be interpreted as implying for any State, group or individual any right to engage in any activity or perform any act contrary to

the Charter of the United Nations or to the Declaration of Principles of International Law on Friendly Relations and cooperation among States in accordance with the Charter of the United Nations.

5. Indigenous peoples have the collective right to exist in peace and security as distinct peoples and to be protected against genocide, as well as the individual rights to life, physical and mental integrity, liberty and security of person.

6. Indigenous peoples have the collective and individual right to maintain and develop their distinct ethnic and cultural characteristics and identities, including the right to self-identification.

7. Indigenous peoples have the collective and individual right to be protected from cultural genocide, including the prevention of the redress for:

    a) Any act which has the aim or effect of depriving them of their integrity as distinct societies, or of their cultural or ethnic characteristics or identities;

    b) Any form of forced assimilation or integration by imposition or other cultures or ways of life;

    c) Dispossession of their lands, territories or resources;

    d) Any propaganda directed against them.

8. Indigenous peoples have the right to revive and practice their cultural identity and traditions, including the right to maintain, develop and protect the past, present and future manifestations of their cultures, such as archaeological and historical sites and structures, artifacts, designs, ceremonies, technology and

works of art, as well as the right to the restitution of cultural, religious and spiritual property taken from them without their free and informed consent on in violation of their own laws.

9. Indigenous peoples have the right to manifest, practice and teach their own spiritual and religious traditions, customs and ceremonies, the right to maintain, protect and have access in privacy to religious and cultural sites; the right to use and control of ceremonial objects; and the right to the repatriation of human remains.

10. Indigenous peoples have the right to revive, use, develop, promote and transmit to future generations their own languages, writing systems and literature, and to designate and maintain their own names of communities, places and persons. States shall take effective measure to ensure that Indigenous peoples can understand and be understood in political, legal and administrative proceedings, where necessary through the provision of interpretation or by other effective means.

11. Indigenous peoples have the right to all levels and forms of education, including access to their own languages, and the right to establish and control their own education systems and institutions. Resources shall be provided by the State for these purposes.

12. Indigenous peoples have the right to have the dignity and diversity of their cultures, histories, traditions and aspirations reflected in all forms of education and public information. States shall take effective measure to eliminate prejudices and to foster tolerance, understanding and good relations.

13. Indigenous peoples have the right to the use of and access to all forms of mass media in their own languages. States shall take effective measures to this end.

14. Indigenous peoples have the right to adequate financial and technical assistance, from States and through international cooperation, to pursue freely their own political, economic, social, cultural and spiritual development, and for the enjoyment of the rights contained in the declaration.

15. Indigenous peoples have the right to recognition of their distinctive and profound relationship with the total environment of the lands, territories and resources which they have traditionally occupied or otherwise used.

16. Indigenous peoples have the collective and individual right to own, control and use the lands and territories they have traditionally occupied or otherwise used. This includes the right to the full recognition of their own laws and customs, land-tenure systems and institutions for the management of resources, and the right to effective measures by States to prevent any interference with or encroachment upon these rights. Nothing in the foregoing shall be interpreted as restricting the development of self-government and self-management arrangements not tied to indigenous territories and resources.

17. Indigenous peoples have the right to the restriction or, where this is not possible, to just and fair compensation for lands and territories which have been confiscated, occupied, used or damaged without their free and informed consent. Unless otherwise freely agreed upon by the peoples concerned, compensation shall preferably take the form of lands and territories of quality, quantity and legal status at least equal to those which were lost.

18. Indigenous peoples have the right to protection and, where appropriate, the rehabilitation of the total environment and productive capacity of their lands and territories, and the right to adequate assistance including international cooperation to this end. Unless otherwise freely agreed upon by the peoples concerned, military activities and the storage or disposal of hazardous materials shall not take place in their lands and territories.

19. Indigenous peoples have the right to special measures for protection, as intellectual property, of their traditional cultural manifestations, such as literature, designs, visual and performing arts, seeds, genetic resources medicine and knowledge of the useful properties of fauna and flora.

20. The right to maintain and develop within their areas of lands and other territories their traditional economic structures, institutions and ways of life, to be

secure in the enjoyment of their own traditional means of subsistence, and to engage freely in their traditional and other economic activities, including hunting, fresh-and salwater fishing, herding, gathering, lumbering and cultivation, without adverse discrimination. In no case may an Indigenous people be deprived of its means of subsistence. The right to just and fair compensation if they have been so deprived.

21. The right to special State measures for the immediate, effective and continuing improvement of their social and economic conditions, with their consent, that reflect their own priorities.

22. The right to determine, plan and implement all health, housing and other social and economic programs affecting them, and as far as possible to develop, plan and implement such programs through their own institutions.

23. The right to participate on an equal footing with all other citizens and without adverse discrimination in the political, economic, social and cultural life of the State and to have their specific character duly reflected in the legal system and in political and socio-economic and cultural institutions, including in particular proper regard to and recognition of Indigenous laws and customs.

24. The right to participate fully at the state level, through representatives chosen by themselves, in decision-making about and implementations of all national and international matters which may affect their rights, life and destiny, including the right of Indigenous peoples to be involved, through appropriate procedures, determined in conjunction with them in devising any laws or administrative measures that may affect them directly, and to obtain their free and informed consent through implementing such measures. State have the duty to guarantee the full exercise of these rights.

25. The collective right to autonomy in matters relating to their own internal and local affairs, including education, information, mass median, culture, religion, health, housing, social welfare, traditional and other economic management activities, land and resources administration and the environment, as well as internal taxation for financing these autonomous functions.

26. The right to decide upon the structure of their autonomous institutions, to select the membership of such institutions according to their own procedures, and to determine the membership of the Indigenous people concerned for these purposes; States have the duty, where the peoples concerned so desire, to recognize such institutions and their memberships through the legal systems and political institutions of the State.

27. The right to determine the responsibilities of individuals to their own community, consistent with universally recognized human rights and fundamental freedoms.

28. The right to maintain and develop traditional contacts, relations and cooperation, including cultural and social exchanges and trade, with their own kith and kin across State boundaries and the obligation of the State to adopt measures to facilitate such contacts.

29. The right to claim that States honour treaties and other agreements concluded with Indigenous peoples, and to submit any disputes that may arise in this matter to competent national or international bodies.

30. The individual and collective right to access to and prompt decision by mutually acceptable and fair procedures for resolving conflicts and disputes and any infringement, public and private, between States and Indigenous peoples, groups or individuals. These procedures should include, as appropriate, negotiations, mediation, arbitration, national courts and international and regional human rights review and complaints mechanisms.

31. These rights constitute the minimum standards for the survival and the well-being of the Indigenous peoples of the world.

32. Nothing in this Declaration may interpreted as implying for any State, group or individual any right to engage in any activity or to perform any act aimed at the destruction of any of the rights and freedoms set forth herein.

Paragraphs suggested by the Chairpersons/Rapporteur for consideration for inclusion without prejudice for their placement.

Indigenous peoples have the right to special protection in periods of armed conflict. States shall observe international standards for the protection of civilian populations in circumstances of emergency and conflict, and shall not:

a) Recruit Indigenous people against their will into the armed forces and in particular, for use against other Indigenous peoples,

b) Force Indigenous people to abandon their land and territories and means of subsistence and relocate them in special centres for military purposes.

Indigenous peoples have the right to retain and develop their customary laws and legal systems where these are not incompatible with fundamental rights defined by international human rights standards.

Indigenous peoples shall not be forcibly removed from their lands or territories. Where relocation occurs it shall be with the free and informed consent of the Indigenous peoples concerned and after agreement on a fair and just compensation and, where possible, the option of return.

MEMORIAL

To Sir Wilfred Laurier, Premier of the Dominion of Canada
From the Chiefs of the Shuswap, Okanagan and Couteau Tribes of British Columbia
Presented at Kamloops, B.C., August 25, 1910

Dear Sir and Father, We take this opportunity of your visiting Kamloops to speak a few words to you. We welcome you here, and we are glad we have met you in our country. We want you to be interested in us, and to understand more fully the conditions under which we live. We expect much of you as the head of this great Canadian nation, and feel confident that you will see that we receive fair and honourable treatment. Our confidence in you has increased since we have noted of late the attitude of your government towards the Indian rights movement of this country and we hope that with your help our wrongs may at last be righted. We speak to you the more freely because you are a member of the white race with whom we first became acquainted, and which we call in our tongue "real whites." One hundred years next year they came amongst us here at Kamloops and erected a trading post. After the other whites came to this country in 1858 we differentiated them from the first whites as their manners were so much different, and we applied the term "real whites" to the latter (viz., the fur-traders of the Northwest and Hudson Bay companies!) as the great majority of the companies employees were French speaking, the term latterly became applied by us as a designation for the whole French race. The "real whites" we found were good people. We could depend on their word, and we trusted and respected them. They did not interfere with us nor attempt to break up our tribal organizations, laws and customs. They did not try to force their conceptions of things on us to our harm. Nor did they stop us from catching fish, hunting, etc. They never tried to steal or appropriate our country, nor take our food an life from us. They acknowledged our ownership of the country, and treated our chiefs as men. They were the first to find us in this country. We never asked them to come here, but nevertheless we treated them kindly and hospitably and helped them all we could. They had made themselves (as it were) our guests. We treated them as such, and then waited to see what they would do. As we found they did us no harm our friendship with them became lasting. Because of this we have a warm heart to the French at the present day. We expect good from Canada. When they first came among us there were only Indians here. They found the people of each tribe supreme in their own territory, and having tribal boundaries known and recognized by all. The country of each tribe was just the same as a very large farm or ranch (belonging to all the people of the tribe) from which they gathered their food. On it they had game which they hunted for food and clothing, etc.; fish which they got in plenty for food; grass and vegetation on which their horses grazed and the game lived, and much of which furnished materials for manufactures, etc.; stone which furnished pipes, utensils; and tools, etc.; trees which furnished firewood, materials for houses and utensils; plants, roots, seeds, nuts and berries which grew abundantly and were gathered in their season just the same as the crops on a ranch, and used for food; minerals, shells, etc., which were used for ornament and for paints, etc.; water which was free to all. Thus fire, water, food, clothing and all the necessaries of life were obtained in abundance from the lands of each tribe, and all the people had equal rights of access to everything they required. You will see the ranch of each tribe was the same as its life, and without it the people could not have lived. Just 52 years ago the other whites came to this country. They found us just the same as the first or "real whites" had found us, only we had larger bands of horses, had some cattle, and in many places we cultivated the land. They found us happy, healthy, strong and numerous. Each tribe was still living in its own "house" or in other words on its own "ranch." No one interfered with our rights, nor disputed our possession of our own "houses" and "ranches," viz., our homes and lives. We were friendly and helped these whites also, for had we not learned the first whites had done us no harm? Only when some of them killed us we revenged on them. Then we thought there are some bad ones among them, but surely on the whole they must be good. Besides they are the queen's people. And we had already heard the great things about the queen from the "real whites." We expected her subjects would do us no harm, but rather improve us by giving us knowledge, and enabling us to do some of the wonderful things they could do. At first they looked only for gold. We knew the latter was our property, but as we did not use it much nor need it to live by we did not object to their searching for it. They told us, "Your country is rich and you will be made wealthy by our coming. We wish just to pass over your lands in quest of gold." Soon they saw the country was good, and some of them made up their minds to settle in it. They commenced to take up pieces of land here and there. They told us they wanted only the use of these pieces of land for a few years, and then would hand them back to us in an improved condition; meanwhile they would give us some of the products they raised for the loan of our land. Thus they commenced to enter our "houses," or live on our "ranches." With us when a person enters our house he becomes our guest, and we must treat him hospitably as long as he shows no hostile intentions. At the same time we expect him to return to us equal treatment for what he receives. Some of our chiefs said, "These people wish to be partners with us in our country. We must, therefore, be the same as brothers to them, and live as one family. We will share equally in everything—half and half—in land, water and timber, etc. What is ours will be theirs, and what is theirs will be ours. We will help each other to be great and good." The whites made a government in Victoria—perhaps the queen made it. We have heard it stated both ways. Their chiefs dwelt there. At this time they did not deny the Indian tribes owned the whole country and everything in it. They told us we did. We Indians were hopeful. We trusted the whites and waited patiently for their chiefs to declare their intentions toward us and our lands. We knew what had been done in the neighbouring states, and we remembered what we had heard about the queen being so good to the Indians and that her laws carried out by her chiefs were always just and better than the American laws. Presently chiefs (government officials, etc.) commenced to visit us, and had talks with some of our chiefs. They told us to have no fear, and queen's laws would prevail in this country, and everything would be well for the Indians here. They said a very large reservation would be staked off for us (southern interior tribes) and the tribal lands outside of this reservation the government would buy from us for white settlement. They let us think this would be done soon, and meanwhile until this reserve was set apart, and our lands settled for, they assure us we would have perfect freedom of travelling and camping and the same liberties as from time immemorial to hunt, fish, graze and gather our food supplies wherever we desired; also that all trails, land, water, timber, etc., would be as free of access to us as formerly. Our chiefs were agreeable to these propositions, so we waited for treaties to be made, and everything settled. We had never known white chiefs to break their word so we trusted. In the meanwhile white settlement progressed. Our chiefs held us in check. They said, "Do nothing against the whites. Something we do not understand retards them from keeping their promise. They will do the square thing by us in the end." What have we received for our good faith, friendliness and patience? Gradually as the whites of this country became more and more powerful, and we less and less powerful, they little by little changed their policy towards us, and commenced to put restrictions on us. Their government or chiefs have taken every advantage of our friendliness, weakness and ignorance to impose on us in every way. They treat us as subjects without any agreement to that effect, and force their laws on us without our consent, and irrespective of whether they are good for us or not. They say they have authority over us. They have broken down our old laws and customs (no matter how good) by which we regulated ourselves. They laugh at our chiefs and brush them aside. Minor affairs amongst ourselves, which do not affect them in the least, and which we can easily settle better than they can, they drag into our courts. They enforce their own laws one way for the rich white man, one way for the poor white, and yet another for the Indian. They have knocked down (the same as) the posts of all the Indian tribes. They say there are no lines, except what they make. They have taken possession of all the Indian country and claim it as their own. Just the same as taking the "house" or "ranch" and, therefore, the life every Indian tribe into their possession. They have never consulted us in any of these matters, nor made any agreement, nor signed any papers with us. They have stolen our lands and everything on them and continue to use same for their own purposes. They treat us as less than children, and allow us no say in anything. They say the Indians know nothing, and own nothing, yet their power and wealth has come from our belongings. The queen's law which we believe guaranteed us our rights, the B.C. Government has trampled under foot. This is how our guests have treated us—the brothers we received hospitably in our house. After a time when they saw that our patience might be exhausted and that we might cause trouble if we thought all the land was to be occupied by whites they set aside many small reservations for us here and there over the country. This was their proposal not ours, and we never accepted these reservations as settlement for anything, nor did we sign any papers or make any treaties about same. They thought we would be satisfied with this, but we never have been satisfied and never will be until we get our rights. We thought the setting apart of these reservations was the commencement of some scheme they had evolved for our benefit, and that they would now continue until they had more than fulfilled their promises but although we have waited long we have been disappointed. We have always felt the injustice done us, but we did not know how to obtain redress. We knew it was useless to go to war. What would we do? Even your government at Ottawa, into whose charge we had been handed by the B.C. Government, gave us no enlightenment. We had no powerful friends. The Indian agents and Indian office at Victoria appeared to neglect us. Some offers of help in the way of agricultural implements, schools, medical attendance, aid to the aged, etc., from the Indian department were at first refused by many of our chiefs or were never petitioned for, because for a time we thought the Ottawa and Victoria governments were the same as one, and these things would be charged against us and rated as payment for our land, etc. Thus we got along the best way we could and asked for nothing. For a time we did not feel the stealing of our lands, etc. very heavily. As the country was sparsely settled we still had considerable liberty in the way of hunting, fishing, grazing, etc., over by far the most of it. However, owing to increased settlement, etc. in late years this has become changed, and we are being more and more restricted to our reservations, which in most places are unfit or inadequate to maintain us. Except we can get fair play we can see we will go to the wall, and most of us be reduced to beggary or to continuous wage slavery. We have also learned lately that the British Columbia government claims absolute ownership of our reservations, which means that we are practically landless. We only have a loan of those reserves in life rent, or at the option of the B.C. Government. Thus we find ourselves without any real home in this our own country. In a petition signed by fourteen of our chiefs and sent to your Indian department, July 1908, we pointed out the disabilities under which we labour owing to the inadequacy of most of our reservations, some having hardly any good land, others, no irrigation water, etc.; our limitations re pasture lands for stock owing to fencing of so-called government lands by whites; the severe restrictions put on us lately by the government re hunting and fishing; the depletion of salmon by over fishing of the whites, and other matters affecting us. In many places we are debarred from camping, travelling, gathering roots and obtaining wood and water as heretofore. Our people are fined and imprisoned for breaking the game and fish laws and using the same game and fish which we were told would always be ours for food. Gradually we are becoming regarded as trespassers over a large portion of this our country. Our old people say, "How are we to live. If the government takes our food from us they must give us other food in its place." Conditions of living have been thrust on us which we did not expect, and which we consider in great measure unnecessary and injurious. We have no grudge against the white race as a whole nor against the settlers, but we want to have an equal chance with them of making a living. We welcome them to this country. It is not in most cases their fault. They have taken up and improved and paid for their lands in good faith. It is their government which is to blame by heaping up injustice on us. But it is also their duty to see their government does right by us, and gives us a square deal. We condemn the whole policy of the B.C. Government towards the Indian tribes of this country as utterly unjust, shameful and blundering in every way. We denounce same as being the main cause of the unsatisfactory condition of Indian affairs in this country and of animosity and friction with the whites. So long as what we consider justice is withheld from us, so long will dissatisfaction and unrest exist among us, and we will continue to struggle to better ourselves. For the accomplishment of this end we and other Indian tribes of this country are now uniting and we ask the help of yourself and your government in this fight for our rights. We believe it is not the desire nor policy of your government that these conditions should exist. We demand that our land question be settled, and ask that treaties be made between the government and each of our tribes, in the same manner as accomplished with the Indian tribes of the other provinces of Canada, and the neighbouring parts of the United States. We desire that every matter of importance to each tribe be a subject of treaty, so we may have a definite understanding with the government on all questions of moment between us and them. In a declaration made last month, and signed by twenty-four of our chiefs (a copy of which has been sent to your Indian department) we have stated our position on these matters. Now we sincerely hope you will carefully consider everything we have herewith brought before you and that you will recognize the disadvantages we labour under, and the darkness of the outlook for us if these questions are not speedily settled. Hoping you have had a pleasant sojourn in this country, and wishing you a good journey home we remain.

Yours very sincerely,

The Chiefs of the Shuswap, Okanagan, and Couteau or Thompson tribes.-Per their secretary, J.A. Teit.

Tribe or Band	Name	No	Where Situated	Acres	Remarks
Nicola (Upper)	Nicola Lake	1	Kamloops division of Yale district, on the eastern shore of Nicola lake, at its head, in townships 96 and 97.	2692	The Lower Nicola reserves were surveyed in 1879. 200 inches of water recorded from Nicola river.
"	Hamilton's Creek Fishery or Quilchena	2	Kamloops division of Yale district, on the eastern shore of Nicola lake at the mouth of Hamilton's or Quilchana creek, in township 97.	60	50 inches of water recorded from Quilchana creek.
"	Douglas Lake	3	Kamloops division of Yale district, at the lower end of Douglas lake, partly in township 96.	23047	300 inches of water recorded from Spahomin creek. 100 inches from lake at head of Lauder creek. 50 inches from a spring on southwest side of reserve.
"	Spahomin Creek	4	Kamloops division of Yale district, on Spahomin creek about seven miles from its mouth.	320	50 inches of water recorded from Spahomin creek.
"	Chapperon Lake	5	Kamloops division of Yale district, on the western shore of Chapperon lake.	725	50 inches of water recorded from Murray creek.
"	Chapperon Creek Fishery	6	Kamloops division of Yale district, on Upper Chapperon creek, about three quarters of a mile from its mouth.	15	25 inches of water recorded from Upper Chapperon creek.
"	Salmon Lake	7	Kamloops division of Yale district, on the trail from Nicola to Grand Prarie.	172	Reserves Nos. 1 to 7 were allotted by CommissionSproat, Sept. 28, 1878, they were surveyed in 1879.
"	Spahomin Creek	8	Kamloops division of Yale district, between reserves Nos. 3 and 4.	3857	Allotted by Commissioner O'Reilly, Oct. 10, 1889. Surveyed 1894. Final confirmation, May 7, 1895.

Tribe or Band	Name	No	Where Situated	Acres	Remarks
Okanagan	Okanagan	1	Osoyoos division of Yale district, at the head of Okanagan lake.	25539	100 inches of water recorded from Siwash creek. 100 inches from Six Mile creek. 35 inches from Louis creek. 75 inches from White Man's creek.
"	Otter Lake	2	Osooyoos division of Yale district, on the shore of Otter lake, in section 23, township 7.	62	
"		3	Osooyoos division of Yale district, the southwest quarter section 13, township 7.	160	
"	Swan Lake	4	Osoyoos division of Yale district, in osections 26 and 35, township 8, on the northern shore of Swan lake.	68	Allotted by the Joint Reserve Commission, October 15, 1877. Surveyed, 1880.
"	Long Lake	5	Osooyoos division of Yale district, on the northern shore of Long lake, a portion of section 22, township 9.	128	
"	Priest's Valley	6	Osooyoos division of Yale district, at the head of the South Arm of Okanagan lake, in section 30, township9.	83	
"	Duck Lake	7	Osooyoos division of Yale distritct, on the northern shore of Duck lake, in townships 20 and 23.	457	Allotted by the Joint Reserve Commission, Oct. 15, 1877. Surveyed, 1880.
"	Mission Creek	8	Osooyoos division of Yale district, on the banks of Mission creek. Portions of sections 5,6,7 and 8, township 26.	55	
"	Tsinstikeptum	9	Osoyoos division of Yale district, on the western shore of Okanagan lake, in township 25.	2438	
"		10	Osooyoos division of Yale district, on the western shore of Okanagan lake, 3.5 miles north of reserve No. 9.	800	Allotted by Commissioner O'Reilly, Oct. 19, 1888. Surveyed, 1889. Final confirmation April 28, 1891.

Tribe or Band	Name	No	Where Situated	Acres	Remarks
Osooyoos	Osooyoos	1	Osooyoos division of Yale district, at the head of Osooyoos lake, portions of townships 48, 49, 50 and 51.	32097	50 inches of water recorded from A-tsi-hlak creek, 100 inches from Wolf creek and 300 inches from Gregoire creek.
"	Dog Lake	2	Osooyoos division of Yale district, on the banks of Okanagan river, at the outlet of Dog lake, in township 86.	71	The Osooyoos reserves were allotted by the Joint Reserve Commission, Nov. 21, 1877. Surveyed, 1889. Final confirmation April 28, 1891.
Penticton	Penticton	1	Osooyoos division of Yale district, at the foot of Okanagan lake, partly in township 88.	47829	100 inches of water recorded from Trout creek, 100 inches from Snake creek and 60 inches from Marron creek. Reserve No. 1 was allotted by the Joint Reserve Commission, November 24, 1877. Surveyed, 1889. Final confirmation, July 10, 1895.
"	Timber reserve	2	Osooyoos division of Yale district, township 87, between Okanagan and Dog lakes.	321	Allotted by Commissioner O'Reilly, July 31, 1893. The southern portion of reserve No. 2, as allotted by the Joint Reserve Commission, Nov. 24, 1887, was surrendered, July 10, 1895.
"	Timber reserve	2a	To the west of and adjoining reserve No. 2.	194	Conveyed by Mr. Thomas Ellis to the crown Sept. 21, 1894. Surveyed, 1889. Final confirmation, July 10, 1895.

Tribe or Band	Name	No	Where Situated	Acres	Remarks
Lower Similkameen		1	Osooyoos division of Yale district, on the left bank of the Similkameen river, in sections 4 and 9, township52.	-	Disallowed by the Provincial Government, April 28, 1891. Cancelled by Commissioner O'Reilly, August 9, 1893.
"		2	Osooyoos division of Yale district, on the left bank of the Similkameen	208	
"		3	Osooyoos division of Yale district, on both banks of the Similkameen, adjoining reserve No. 2 on the south.	1750	
"	Narcisse's Farm	4	Osooyoos division of Yale district, on the right bank of the Similkameen river, opposite to reserves Nos. 2 and 3, 9 miles north of the international boundary line.	1854	Forty inches of water recorded from Sintlehahtan creek.
"	Joe Nahumcheen	5	Osooyoos division of Yale district, on both banks of the Similkameen, to the south of and adjoining reserve No 3.	1278	Ten inches of water recorded to be taken out of a spring at the back of Joe Nahumcheen's farm. One hundred inches of water from the Similkameen river.
"	Blind Creek	6	Osooyoos division of Yale district, part of sections 11 and 14, township 52.		
"	Skemeoskuankin	7/8	Osooyoos division of Yale district, on the right bank of the Similkameen river, north of and adjoining the international boundary line.	3800	One hundred inches of water recorded from Skemeoskuankin creek.
"	Alexis	9	Osooyoos division of Yale district, on the left bank of the Similkameen river, five miles above Keremens	429	One hundred inches of water recorded from Achegheptlat creek.

Tribe or Band	Name	No	Where Situated	Acres	Remarks
Lower Similkameen	Ashnola	10	Osooyoos division of Yale district, on the right bank of the Similkameen river, at its confluence with the Ashnola river.	4153	One hundred inches of water recorded from Ashnola river and 50 inches from Jim's creek.
"	"	10a	On the right bank of the Similkameen river, to the north of and adjoining reserve No. 10.	3724	
"	"	10b	On the right bank of the Similkameen river, to the south of and adjoining reserve No. 10.	411	
"	Ashnola John's	11	Osooyoos division of Yale district, on the right bank of the Similkameen river, 13 miles above Keremens.	585	One hundred inches of water recorded from Sinthutsepaskan creek.
"		12	Osooyoos division of Yale district, on Keremens creek, about 14 miles from Keremens, on the Keremens to the Penticton wagon road.	150	Reserves Nos. 1,2,7,8,9,10,11 and 12 were allotted by Commissioner Sproat, October 12, 1878. No. 3 was allotted by Commission O'Reilly, September 22, 1884. Nos. 4, 5 and 6 were allotted by Commissioner O'Reilly, October 30, 1888. Nos. 10a, 10b and 12a were allotted by Commissioner O'Reilly, August 9, 1893.
"		12a	On Keremens creek, to the north and west of reserve No.12, and adjoining the same.	1130	Reserves 7,8,9,10 and 11 finally confirmed, April 28, 1891. Reserves 2,3,4,5,6,12,10a,10b and 12b confirmed, June 8, 1895.
"		12b			Information wasn't available at time of printing.

Tribe or Band	Name	No	Where Situated	Acres	Remarks
Similkameen (Upper)	Vermilion Forks	1	Osooyoos division of Yale district, at Vermillion Forks on the Similkameen river, near Princeton.	21	
"	Chuchuwayha	2	Osooyoos division of Yale district, on the banks of the Similkameen, at 20-Mile creek, 20 miles below Princeton.	4130	200 inches of water recorded from Similkameen river. 100 inches of water recorded from 20 mile creek. 100 inches of water recorded from N-kan-si-ko, Aks spe-papts-in and Chu-chu-way-ha creeks. 100 inches recorded from N-kam-a-hi-nat creek.
"	"	2a	To the west of and adjoining reserve No. 2.	1400	
"	"	2b	On the right bank of the Similkameen to the west of and adjoining reserve No. 2.	175	
"	Wolf Creek or Yakhl-kaywalick	3	Osooyoos division of Yale district, on the right bank of the Similkameen at the mouth of Wolf creek, 9 miles from Princeton.	505	100 inches of water recorded from Wolf creek.
"	Nine Mile Creek	4	Osooyoos division of Yale district, on the left bank of theSimilkameen at the mouth of 9-Mile creek, opposite to reserve No. 3	250	30 inches of water recorded from 9-Mile creek.
"	Lulu	5	Osooyoos division of Yale district, on the left bank of the Similkameen river, about 12 miles distant from the former.	52	100 inches of water recorded from Lula-a-lauh creek

Tribe or Band	Name	No	Where Situated	Acres	Remarks
Similkameen (Upper)		6	Kamloops division of Yale district, on the trail from Princeton to Nicola, and about 12 miles distant from the former.	20	Reserves Nos. 1,5 and 6 allotted by Commissioner Sproat, October 5, 1878.
"	Iltcoola	7	Osooyoos division of Yale district, on the left bank of the Similkameen river, about 11 miles below Princeton.	30	Reserve No. 2 allotted by Commissioner O'Reilly, Oct. 26, 1888. Reserves Nos. 3,4,7. 2a and 2b allotted by Commissioner O'Reilly, August 5, 1893. These reserves have not been surveyed.
Similkameen (Upper), in common.	Pauls's Basin	2	Yale district, on the left bank of the Coldwater river, about 12 miles from its mouth.	1594	100 inches of water recorded from the stream flowing through the reserve.
	Meadow	3	Kamloops division of Yale district, about 4 miles east of reserve No. 1.	42.5	20 inches of water recorded from the stream running into the lake on the reserve. Allotted by Commissioners Sproat, Sept. 11, 1878. Surveyed, 1886. Final confirmation, May 8, 1889.

BIBLIOGRAPHY

Spier, Leslie et al.
The Sinkaietk or Southern Okanagan of Washington. General Series in Anthropology, Number 6, Menasha, Wisconsin, USA, 1938.

Teit, James A.
The Okanagan extracted from The Salishan Tribes of the Western Plateaus. 45th B.A.E. Annual Report, 1927-28

Ray, Verne F.
Native Villages and Groupings of the Columbia Basin- The Lakes/ Sna'itckstkw. The Pacific Northwest Quarterly, vol.XXVII. Seattle, Wash: University of Washington 1936.

Hill-Tout, Charles.
The Salish People. Vol. 1 The Thompson and the Okanagan, edited and introduction by Maud, Ralph. Vancouver: Talonbooks 1978.

Colden, Cadwallader.
The History of the Five Indian Nations of Canada - 1747. Toronto: Coles Publishing Company, 1972.

Francis, R. 1 Douglas et al.
Origins: Canadian History to Confederation. Toronto: Hold, Reinhart & Winston, 1988.

Keenleyside, Hugh L.
Canada & the United States. New York: Alfred A. Knopf, 1952.

Reid, Stewart J.H.; McNaught, Kenneth; Crowe, Harry S.
A Source Book of Canadian History. Don Mills, Ontario: Longman's Canada Ltd., 1964.

McInnis, Edgar.
Canada A Political and Social History Fourth Edition with a final chapter by Michael Horn Toronto: Holt, Reinhart and Winston of Canada Ltd., 1982.

Goulson, Cary F.
Seventeenth Century Canada Source Studies. Toronto: McMillan of Canada, 1970.

Morton, W.L.
The Kingdom of Canada. A General History of Earliest Times. Toronto, Montreal: McClelland and Stewart Ltd., 1963.

Waite, P.B.
Pre-Confederation Canada Historical Document Series, Vol. II. Scarborough, Ontario: Prentice-Hall of Canada Ltd., 1965.

Eccles, W.J.
The Canadian Frontier 1534 - 1960, Revised edition. Albuquerque: University of New Mexico Press, 1969.

Cassidy, Frank.
Aboriginal Title in British Columbia Delgamuukuv the Queen. Proceedings of a Conference September 10, 11, 1991. Lantzville B.C. and Montreal: Oolican Books and Institute for Research on Public Policy, 1992.

Begg, Alexander.
History of British Columbia From Its Earliest Discovery to the Present Time. Toronto: McGraw-Hill Ryerson Ltd. 1972.

Ormsby, Margaret A.
British Columbia: A History. Toronto: MacMillan of Canada Ltd., 1958.

Akrigg and Akrigg, G. P. V. and Helen B.
British Columbia Chronicle 1847 - 1871 Gold and Colonists. Vancouver: Discovery Press, 1977.

Akrigg and Akrigg, G. P. V. and Helen B.
British Columbia Chronicle 1878 - 1846 Adventures by Sea and Land. Vancouver: Discovery Press, 1975.

Ward, W. Peter and McDonald, Robert A. J.
British Columbia: Historical Readings. Vancouver: Douglas and McIntyre Ltd., 1981.

Frideres, James S.
Native People in Canada Contemporary Conflicts. Scarborough, Ontario: Prentice-Hall Canada Inc. 1983.

Cumming, Peter A. and Mickenberg, Neil H. co-editors.
Native Rights in Canada Second Edition. Toronto: General Publishing Co. Ltd. and Indian-Eskimo Association of Canada, 1972.

Clark, Bruce.
Native Liberty, Crown Sovereignty, The Existing Aboriginal Right of Self-Government in Canada. Montreal and Kingston: McGill-Queen's University Press, 1990.

Little Bear, Leroy; and Boldt, Menno; and Long, J. Anthony.
Pathways to Self-Determination Canadian Indians and the Canadian State. Toronto: University of Toronto Press, 1984.

Boldt, Menno; and Long, J. Anthony; associated with Little Bear, Leroy
The Quest for Justice Aboriginal peoples and Aboriginal Rights
Toronto: University of Toronto Press, 1985

Richardson, Boyce introduction by Erasmus, Georges
Drum Beat Anger and Renewal In Indian Country. Toronto: Summerhill press Ltd. 1989.

Galois,R.M., The Indian Rights Association, Native Protest Activity and the "Land Question" in British Columbia, 1903-1916. Native Studies Review, University of Saskatchewan, vol. 8 num.2, 1992.

Prichard, John and Pearson, Norman. Indian Reserve Commission Commanages In British Columbia. A report prepared for the Okanagan Tribal Council. Oct, 1985

Fery and Finlayson, Jules and Roderick.Journals of Sir James Douglas, 1827, 1835, 1840-41, 1843, 1846 - 50, 1852, 1858, 1860, 1861. Transcribed from microfilm by The Bancroft Library, University of California Berkeley.

British Columbia,
Royal Commission on Indian Affairs for the Province of B.C. Proceedings. 4 volumes. Victoria: 1916 and Evidence of the Royal Commission's Meetings. transcribed ver batim 1913.

British Columbia, R. Wolfenden. Papers Connected With the Indian Land Question, 1850-1875. Victoria,1875

British Columbia, Sessional Papers 1871-1924

Canada, Department of Indian Affairs. Indian Reserve Commission, McKinly, Sproat Anderson Reports, Correspondence, Orders-in-council 444,779 and related papers. Central registry. Black Series Western on PABC Microfilm reels 271-361, file 3576 reel 279 and GR 495 and PABC Microfiche Bf-3.

Canada, Department of Indian Affairs. Schedule of Indian Reserves in the Province of British Columbia. Ottawa, 1943

Canada, Special Joint Committee on Claims of the Allied Tribes of British Columbia. Proceedings, reports and evidence. Ottawa 1927

Central Interior Tribal Council of British Columbia. Declarations of the Interior Tribes of British Columbia. Kamloops: CITC, 1982

Davis and Company, Barristers and Solicitors.
Native Law Bulletin, Aborginal Appeals. June 29, 1993

McCarthy Tetrault, Aboriginal Law Group.
Aborginal Rights Decisions Released, R.v. Delgamuukw and Seven Aborignal Fishing and Hunting Appeals. June, 1993

PRINTED IN CANADA